Aurora
TALES OF WINTER DREAMS

Edited by
River Eno
& LCW Allingham

Speculation Publications

ISBN-13: 979-8-9918553-7-2
Ebook: 979-8-9918553-5-8
Executive Editor: River Eno
Editor: LCW Allingham
Assistant Editor : Susan Tulio

Cover Art: LCW Allingham
Book Design and Layout: LCW Allingham
Copyright © 2025 Speculation Publications LLC

Vectors and Illustrations: Envato Elements

Published by Speculation Publications
No part of this book was created by AI

For More Information go to www.speculationpub.com

For Cheryl Cantafio

Table of Contents

Aurora

Foreword
BY RIVER ENO

In *The Epic of Gilgamesh* prophetic dreams foreshadow the story and reveal the will of the gods. Mary Shelley was inspired to write Frankenstein by a waking dream. The Abenaki Great Spirit fell asleep while building the earth on the back of a turtle, and his dreams finished his creation. The goddess Kannon appeared to a monk in his dream, compelling him to create the miraculous Ichimen-Juichimen Kannon. Penelope's dreams prophesize her husband's return and victory in *the Odyssey*. The Dreaming Prophet, Edgar Cayce, received instructions for healing and visions of the future from his dreams.

Winter is a time of rest, reflection, and dreaming of what is to come. Dreams that can convey messages from the gods, from the fey, from the dead, from our higher self and our shadow selves; the part of us that lives deep in our unconscious, the part of us that takes in everything we are seeing, everything that is happening around us and pulls it down deep, swirls it around and tries to make sense of it, like building sculptures in the snow.

Searching for meanings in our dreams—and nightmares—is as innate as the dreaming itself; dissecting the experience and finding the bits and pieces that may reveal a truth; either a truth of self or a truth of circumstance. Studies show that dreams can be a forewarning, and while dreams are indeed an involuntary happening, many believe we have influence over them, at least some of the time.

Aurora: Tales of Winter Dreams is a firm but gentle guide into the dreaming world—the melancholic longing within Cheryl Cantafio's "Winter Seraphim." In "Cold Soup For The Soup Collector" by Fendi S. Tulodo, Jara journeys through a kaleidoscope of fever dreams to bring her lost brother home.

"The Salt of It," by Nicole Walsh, a lonely girl comes of age and learns of heartbreak and ancestral obligations. And Bella Chacha's unearthly, "Dreaming of Dibia Snow," watches Adaobi wander through the glass forest, where souls walk without a body, searching for a way out.

Through Finna, in JM Cyrus' "A Winter like We Dreamt Before," the importance of a life well lived outside of dreaming goes hand in hand with perseverance and forgiveness. Jordan Bianchi's, "Flightless of the Way to the North," gives our dreams space to rise, and grace if they happen to fall along the way.

Since I was a child I've loved everything about dreaming, even nightmares. I love to wake up feeling like I've been to another place or time. I long for dreams that are tangible with scent, touch and sound, waking abruptly with an idea for a story or feeling as if I were being told a secret that would reveal itself when I deciphered the cornucopia of images I was shown. And I learned, at times, I can take charge of my night wanderings with lucid dreaming and astral projection—two mediums that are difficult to learn, but I highly recommend.

The contemplation of the long nights of winter energizes me. And while some feel lonely in the darkness, I feel comforted by what greets me there, uplifted by the quiet and eager for the chance to learn from my, sometimes bewildering, inner voice.

"Aurora: Tales of Winter Dreams" was born from a need to make sense of the strange musings of our sleeping imaginations, the desire to find the meaning in the sometimes thorny haystack that is our unconscious mind. Because if we listen, dreams help us grow, by planting seeds that blossom when the cold days of slumber are over, and the sun shines brightly again.

Peace and Shadow,

Wintry Seraphim
BY CHERYL CANTAFIO

i whimper a prayer in the frost-filled air: *amen*
my stomach beats to the furious drums of hunger
i watch them from the iris, snowdrop, and cyclamen
my body yearning for the days when i was younger

my stomach beats to the furious drums of hunger
i lie dormant as my final fantasy takes flight
my body yearning for the days when i was younger
i smile as my friends defy convention and frostbite

i lie dormant as my final fantasy takes flight
my heart leaps at the chance to play with them in the snow
i smile as my friends forgo convention and frostbite
my grave girdled by snow angels – *look at them go*

my heart leaps at the chance to play with them in the snow
i watch them from the iris, snowdrop, and cyclamen
my grave girdled by snow angels – *look at them go*
i whisper a prayer in the frost-filled air: *amen*

Winter Solstice Ritual

CM Riddle
High Priestess

Winter Solstice Ritual

BY CM RIDDLE

Ushering in the Elemental Directions at Winter Solstice for a joyful new year

This is an original Winter Solstice ritual written by Tina Deason, High Priestess of the Iseum of Mary Isis. We are a non-profit organization, established in 1998, located in Northern California. We are a congregation of ordained Priestesses. Our mission includes devotion to women's spiritual growth and to celebrate, protect and honor all of life by embracing Mother Nature and all her relations.

In ancient times, before the popular use of the Gregorian Calendar, ancestors from many locations across the earth gathered to celebrate the "return of the sun," and with it, a new year.

Ancient people recognized the changing of the seasons and noted each took place around a quarter of the way of the earth's annual travel around the sun. Today we note these dates as the: Vernal Equinox around March 21st, which represents East and birth.
Summer Solstice, around June 21st, which represents South and life.

Autumnal Equinox near September 21st, which represents West and death,
followed by Winter Solstice representing North and re-birth, on or about 21st of December.

The Winter Solstice brought true darkness. Because the earth moved so far from the sun, and without artificial lighting, the days grew shorter, and the nights grew longer. The dark time carried fear. Fear of cold, starvation and sickness, especially for the elderly and the young. Some people may have doubted the sun would grow strong again.

Because the Winter Solstice also marked the return of the light (sun), many people, tribes and communities gathered with hope for this new cycle. A festival, sometimes called Yule—an old Norse word for wheel—welcomed earth's new journey around the sun. This rotation of the year is often called the "Wheel of the Year" in pagan practice.

To honor ancient traditions, you may choose to celebrate the Winter Solstice with a ritual. By devoting a blessing to each of the upcoming seasons you will acknowledge its powerful energies. Activating your desires in conjunction with the earth's journey enhances connection to Earth, and all who live upon it.

This ritual may be used by solitaries or groups.

You will need:
- Fireplace, fire pit or BBQ, which is already lit
- Four pinecones
- These instructions with the blessings to recite

What you'll do:
One person may lead, or group members may be assigned a pinecone for a specific element. Recite the blessing while standing at the appropriate location for each direction, East, South, etc.. Once the blessing is said, they will toss the pinecone into the fire.

Begin by gathering around the fire.

The leader will say: "Blessed Be the Winter Solstice; Blessed Be the Light. We gather to invoke our winter wishes to take flight!"

Take the first pinecone and say: "By the dawn of the East, we open ourselves to dream, inviting inspiration for all things we do in the new year." Then toss the pinecone into the fire.

Take the second pinecone and say: "By the warmth of the South, we develop empathy and compassion for all living beings in this new year." Then toss the pinecone into the fire.

Take the third pinecone and say: "With banishing powers of the West, we release negative emotions and embrace love in the new year." Then toss the pinecone into the fire.

Take the last pinecone and say: "By the wisdom of the North, we cast out fear creating room for courage in all things we do this new year." Then toss the pinecone into the fire.

The leader will say: "As the pinecones burn, so do your fears and dread. Your dreams and wishes rise with the smoke, sending them to the heavens.

Suggest everyone take a moment to gaze at the fire and, if they desire, envision what a joyful new year means to them.

The leader will say: "And so it is! Great blessings to you, and a

Merry Winter Solstice to All!

It is customary to share refreshments and socialize after a ritual.

Cold Soup for the Sleep Collector

BY FENDY S. TULODO

No one really knows where your dreams go when you drop them. Not the good ones, wrapped in gold fog, or the bad ones, soaked and shivering in the corners of your mind. But down there—way past where stories like to stay—something waits with a spoon and a map that only shows regrets.

Jara had stopped sleeping properly the winter her brother vanished. Not died—vanished. Like a curtain pulled back, and he was no longer there. No accident. No phone call. Just *nothing*. She'd gone to bed one night in her twin-sized rental room, where the radiator sounded like old bones clapping, and when she woke, it was like a whole chapter of her life had skipped a page.

For months, she tried everything. Sleep clinics. Hypnosis. Even chewing valerian root soaked in gin (it only made her cry into a hotel pillow in Minsk). Her mind became a broken film projector, playing pieces of someone else's dreams.

But tonight…no. Tonight was different.

She took the tram out of the city at midnight, her breath fogging up the scratched window, her boots too light for the snow. Past the frozen zoo and the tunnel of flickering lights, until she reached the old Aquarium Museum. It had closed years ago after a penguin riot—local myth, mostly. But what mattered was what lived below it now. The Dream Station.

She pushed through the rusty service door marked *OUT OF ORDER*, past wet pipes and graffiti that hummed in languages her grandmother used to mumble before dementia took her words. At the bottom of the stairwell: a long hallway lit by upside-down candles and a vending machine that sold memories in blister packs.

A man with three neckties and no nose looked up from his clipboard. "First time?"

"First time," Jara said.

"You here to drop a dream or pick one up?"

"Neither. I want mine back."

He squinted, then handed her a token the color of throat lozenges. "Then you're looking for the Collector. Platform 0. Don't eat anything unless it sings. Don't name anything unless it bleeds."

She nodded. Didn't ask. She was too tired for logic.

The train wasn't really a train.

It moved like guilt—slow and hot in the lungs. The cabin was made of chipped porcelain, like someone had tried to build a dining room out of a nightmare. Around her sat other passengers, none making eye contact. A girl fed sleep spores to a stuffed rabbit with surgical tape on its mouth. A man in a gold suit sobbed quietly into a pillow that blinked.

The ceiling was a film screen. Projecting people's regrets. Jara watched one loop of a woman burning letters she never sent, again and again, her hands shaking more with each replay. There were no conductors. No doors. The windows only showed snow swirling like it was angry.

A voice spoke inside her ear. Not near—inside.

"If your dream is not returned, compensation will be extracted in moments that taste like pennies."

She swallowed and tasted metal. Then…the Soup Collector arrived.

He came pushing a dented food cart, steaming and reeking of boiled wool and mint. His eyes were egg yolks. His fingers…mismatched. Like he'd borrowed some from other people and forgot to return them. The cart was stacked with lidded bowls, each labeled with an emotion.

He stopped in front of Jara. Tilted his head like a crow confused by a mirror.

"Name?"

She didn't answer.

He sniffed her hair. "Mmm. Abandonment. A hint of unreliable narration. You're here for retrieval, aren't you?"

"I want the dream you took from me," she said.

He cackled. It sounded like knives dancing on glass. "Oh, sweet dropper. *They're not taken. They're cooked.*"

He pulled back a curtain on the cart. Inside: a swirling broth of dreams—faces dissolving into ink, sounds melting into feelings. One bubble popped, and the smell of a first kiss came out. Another burst with a scream she recognized as her mother's.

He handed her a ladle. "If you find yours, it's yours again. But only if you offer something equal. You know the rule."

"The hell you after?" she breathed out.

He stepped in too close—now she saw dead things dancing behind his teeth.

"Your worst holiday memory."

Volgograd, 2012.

Jara was supposed to be in Tallinn. Instead, her visa got delayed, and she was stranded in Russia with a suitcase full of tropical clothes, and no hotel room. She took the only train heading anywhere warmer and ended up in Volgograd during a blizzard.

The snow was vicious. Her scarf tore off in the wind. Her boots soaked through in minutes. By the time she reached the inn, her lips were blue. Inside: a funeral was happening. Wrong town. Wrong grief. But she stayed. She drank the broth. She held an old woman's hand who thought she was her niece. She even cried when the coffin closed, not for the stranger, but because it was easier than crying for herself.

The Soup Collector inhaled the memory with his teeth, like slurping fog. "Delicious. Underprepared misery. With real loneliness. Rare vintage."

He dropped something into her hands. A small glowing jar. Inside: a scene.

Her brother. Smiling. On a yellow sled, rushing down the hill near their childhood apartment. She was chasing him. Laughing. She could hear their father's voice in the background, calling for hot cocoa.

Her knees buckled.

"Is it real?" she whispered.

"It's yours," he said. "Which isn't always the same thing."

The train doors, which hadn't been there a moment before, hissed open.

Jara stepped off onto a platform made of old diary pages. She didn't look back.

She woke up in her own bed at 3:14 AM.

Outside, the world was still. Her dog—dead five years— barked once from the kitchen. The radiator sang a song she knew but had no name for. On the nightstand sat the jar, now empty but warm.

She opened her mouth and exhaled snow.

Not the cold kind. The good kind.

Three days after she got the dream back, things started to go…strange. Not awful. Not blood-in-the-bathtub strange. Just tilted. Like the world had been taken off its hinge by someone in a hurry.

Jara began hearing laughter where there was no one. Not creepy horror movie giggles—just soft, familiar ones. Her brother's, mostly. Once in the shower, once behind the fridge, and once from her coat pocket. She'd reach into it and find nothing but lint and a breath that didn't belong to her.

She didn't tell anyone. Not her ex-boyfriend who still emailed her articles about sleep hygiene. Not her therapist, who smelled like thyme and always asked the wrong questions. Not even the neighbor boy who sometimes knocked just to ask if ghosts get bored.

She figured it was a side effect. After all, she got her dream back. That should've been enough. But no one warns you that dreams, once cooked and returned, start to hatch.

On the fourth night, her walls peeled open.

Not literally. Not with plaster and nails. But she woke up and realized her bedroom was no longer a bedroom. The wallpaper had become moving fabric, like lungs exhaling. The bed stretched long and narrow, turning into a corridor. A soft red glow pulsed at the far end.

She didn't scream. You only scream when you don't already know.

Barefoot, she walked. The floor was warm, too warm. Like sun on a grave. The corridor narrowed until she had to crawl. Then squeeze. Then fold herself.

When she popped through the other side, she was standing in the cafeteria of her old primary school.

Tables were upside-down. The clock was running backward. And at the center sat a boy in a red hoodie, sipping soup from a bowl too big for his hands.

"...Beni?" she asked.

He looked up.

"You're late," he said. "Soup's getting cold."

They sat across from each other. No one else was around, unless you counted the janitor made entirely of chewing gum who floated near the ceiling.

She stared at the boy. Her brother. But younger. Nine, maybe ten.

"You're not real," she said, not sure if it was for him or herself.

"You brought me back. You fed the Collector. I'm as real as your worst memory, which is very real." He slurped. "You taste different now."

"I want to know where you really are," she said. "If this is just—just some leftover scrap—"

Beni shook his head. "No scraps. I'm still here. But only here. In these stitched-up places."

She wanted to reach across, but her arms wouldn't move. The dream had rules.

"You remember the hill?" he asked. "The sled?"

"Yes. I chased you. Dad was yelling something stupid. You laughed so hard you peed your pants."

He grinned. "Still do."

They both laughed, and it hurt. Like pressing on a healed bruise. Like kissing a ghost.

A bell rang.

The room flickered like a bad signal. The soup evaporated. So did Beni.

And just like that, she was back in her bed, mouth full of snow again.

But this time it was bitter.

After that, she didn't go outside for six days.

She kept hearing other dreams knocking. Ones she never invited. A woman on the phone asking about penguins. A hand that reached from the drain and dropped a ticket to a cinema that burned down in 1998.

Sleep came in pieces. No longer dreams—just visits. Glimpses. The dream soup had changed something fundamental. Not just inside her. But around her. The line was gone. Now the dreams knew her address.

On the seventh day, she made a decision.

She would go back.

There was only one problem.

The Station was closed.

The Aquarium Museum had been demolished that morning. News said it collapsed in on itself. One janitor claimed he saw a train emerge from the ruins and vanish into a pothole. Another said the air smelled like "grief and lemon tea."

Jara packed a bag. Left a note for no one. Then followed the frost trail back through the parts of the city that didn't make it onto Google Maps. It took her two days, three arguments with old statues, and one fake name to get back to Platform 0.

Only now, it was snowing upward.

The platform had changed.

Where once there were candles, now hung spoons. Hundreds of them. Clinking softly like windchimes. Each one engraved with a name. Hers was missing.

But the train came anyway.

No announcement. Just the sound of a lullaby hummed by an unborn child.

Jara stepped in.

This time, she didn't sit. She stood in the aisle, clutching her bag, staring each dream in the eye. One smiled and removed its face like a hat. Another offered her a peach pit that blinked.

She declined. Politely.

The Soup Collector was waiting.

Same cart. Same steam. But now, his apron was stained with something darker.

"Well, well," he crooned. "The borrower returns. Regret, I presume?"

"I want in," she said. "Not just the taste. The kitchen. The core. I want to find my brother."

He tsk-tsk'd. "You already did."

"No," she said. "I found a version. A loop. I want the original. Whole and unsalted."

His fingers twisted into a fork. "Then you'll have to pay in full."

She reached into her bag and pulled out her worst dream. The real one.

Not Volgograd. Not winter.

It was "the day she almost let go." In a hotel in Rotterdam. Bathtub. Pills. A note that only said, "I'm tired of being tired."

The Collector sniffed it and flinched. "Oof. That's…potent."

"Deal?"

He nodded. Dropped the dream into the broth. The soup screamed. Then sang. Then whistled.

He turned and pointed with his ladle. "Door behind the teeth."

She didn't ask what that meant. She just ran.

The door was a molar the size of a car. She climbed it.

Knocked once.

Inside: the Underdream.

Not quite nightmare. Not quite memory. It looked like a hospital made from childhood. Hallways of soft carpet. Nurses with no eyes. Paintings that melted when she stared too long.

She followed the sound of sleds. Of laughter. Of cocoa boiling over.

She found Beni in a room made of cardboard.

This time, older. Maybe twelve. Sitting in front of a monitor, watching himself.

Loop after loop. Different deaths. Drowning. Fire. Falling.

She stepped in. He didn't turn.

"I'm stuck," he whispered.

"I came to get you."

"You shouldn't have."

"I had to."

He looked at her. Finally. And he was him. Not a version. Not a dream. Just...her brother.

"But I can't leave. I was cooked, remember? Half broth now."

She reached into her chest. Pulled out the only thing left.

Her name.

She handed it to him.

The dream exploded.

Soup everywhere. Screams, laughter, colors she'd never seen before. The world folded. Rebuilt. Collapsed again.

When Jara woke up, it was in her bed.

Snow on the windows.

No jar.

But someone humming in the kitchen.

She walked in and saw Beni, just Beni, pouring cereal.

"We're out of milk," he said.

She smiled, nodded.

Her name was gone now. But she didn't need it.

Not today.

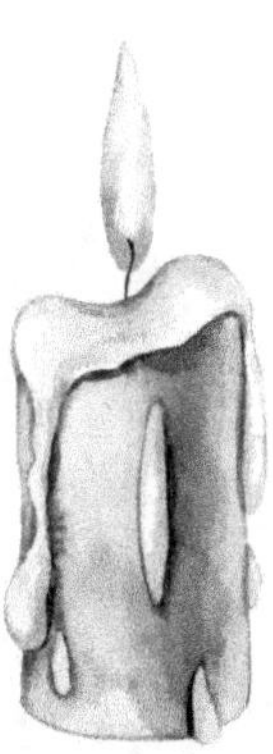

The Salt of It

BY NICOLE WALSH

Many moons ago, a world or two away, there was a tower and a lake and a girl and a long, endless winter. Each morning the girl sat at her window and watched the thin dry leaves on the trees in the courtyard, beneath the press of the mountain. She pulled on wool-lined boots and a heavy coat and walked bare halls, out around the flowerless courtyards, along the hard stony ground of the orchard, circling the mirror-like lake.

The girl's mother lived far above the girl, on a mountain wreathed and ringed with clouds and frost. Most days, the girl could see the mountain, or parts of it, but she could not see her mother's house, so high did it sit amongst the pines and the cliffs.

On occasions, the mother descended to visit the girl. She walked down from the cold and the grey and the ice, wrapped in soaked, wet layers of heavy clothing. The girl knew the woman by her heavy coat and clothing, which she never removed and because the servants told her that this was her mother.

The girl was well cared for. Food was always on the table. The halls, although cold, were lit with torches and fires burned in the hearths. Clothing was mended. Gifts were set before the girl—combs and belts and shoes and toys and books and puzzles. Servants were everywhere, sweeping and tidying and moving busily about. They toiled in the laundry, the kitchen, the field.

The girl never could keep track of their names. Sometimes they spoke at her: how are you? Do you have enough food, enough clothing? Does anyone make you feel uncomfortable?

The same questions, the same answers: fine and yes and yes and no. As the girl grew older, she had questions.

"Where are you from?" she asked a boy.

"Do you live near here?" she asked a girl.

"Did you buy these animals from the markets?" she asked a woman.

"Have you worked other places before this?" she asked a man.

"Is everywhere like this? Is everyone like me?"

The more questions she asked, the less they seemed to respond. They smiled with their mouths but not with their eyes. They avoided her, as if her questions were a wall building between them.

The mother visited at intervals. Once, to tell the girl her father, whom the girl had never met, had died. The statement was set into the space between them, a thing that had little context to the girl. The mother explained it in words, and the words felt like things in the room with them, like ornaments set on shelves around them. The weight and stack of it remained, long after the woman had trekked her way back up to her pines and her cliffs, to her ring of frost and cloud and empty sky.

When the girl became a woman, the mother came to sit with the girl, to make sure she had what she needed, to tell her the facts of the thing.

It was late morning. Clouds curtained the sun. The woman had hugged the girl. The girl had felt the damp in the mother's clothing.

"You are a woman now," the mother said.

A man was found for the girl, a man she may decide to wed.

Her mother descended to tell her this. They would meet, and if he pleased the girl, she could go with him far away, where she might, perhaps, be happy. The blood was a flag of this, a door opened. It would, her mother explained, herald another loss. Of self into wife. Of childhood and home. A loss of this woman, as well, as the girl could only be daughter or wife.

The girl sat for a time beside the cold and the dark of the abandoned well and thought, this perhaps was not a bad thing. There was stone and sky and cold in all places. One chapter seemed the same to her, and there was little holding her here.

Then came another visit. The man chosen for the girl had died. His carriage had over-turned. Fallen into some black, dark ravine. The girl…spared? Abandoned? In the cold shadows of the shortening afternoon, the girl could not tell.

Next came another girl. She climbed into the valley down some goat trail, from a village close by. Her hair was the watery colour of the sun. Her eyes the colour of sky, unscreened by clouds. She brought colour and sunlight into the valley. She was not a part of the mountain. The cold, grey damp had no power over this visitor.

They played together on the paths, up into the streams, along the heights and the depths of the valley. They picked flowers and hunted mushrooms. They lay together, studying the pattern of the leaves—the ones on the forest floor, and those yet to fall.

"Why do you stay?" the visitor asked.

Was there a choice? Something beyond waiting for someone, or something else, to change things?

The girl had no words to explain it. It was a stone, lodged beneath her heart. It was concepts set like ornaments along a shelf. It was her mother, recognisable only by her heaped, wet cloaks and clothing.

"I will take you away," the visitor decided. "I will save you from this shadow."

The girl with the golden hair had kissed her. Or, perhaps she had kissed the girl. It had been such a close thing, the tangle of breath and hearts and gazes, lips so close it was barely a brush to meet.

It changed something. The warmth of those lips, against the cold pallor of the girl's own. Some chill, slipping between them. The cold breath of the mountain. As the visitor pulled back, the girl had seen the shadow of it in her eyes. Grey, across the blue.

The following day the girl's mother descended. Word had come of another death. The visiting girl, fallen somehow into the lake. Drowned.

The mother sat with the daughter a time. The daughter had questions.

"How?" the girl demanded.

"It happens," the woman said.

"I loved her."

"This is how all love ends," the mother said. "Nothing is forever. The deeper you love, the deeper you get hurt."

"My father?" the girl asked.

"Fell and cracked his head."

"Why?"

"Because," the mother said, "he was not here. Where he belonged."

"And, my intended?"

"His eyes were not on the road," the mother explained. "He was not concentrating, not focusing. Not where he should have been."

"And…" the girl could not say her beloved's name.

"You loved her," the mother said. "You let her into your heart, and she broke it."

The girl started to pace.

"This is you," the girl said. "This is, all of it, you."

"I set the truth of it before you," the mother said. "Listen, or do not."

Her mother left.

The girl put on her fur lined boots. She put on her heavy coat. She walked out. She left her mother and her house and her name and her wealth and her home. She walked along the paths above the lake. She climbed between lichen-covered boulders, in between the green slot of them, stroking the thin wiry lichen, where some trace of her friend's touch lingered. She climbed up and up along the path her friend had discovered.

Over the ridge, down the slope, to a village.

Her friend's house. The friend's mother and father and sisters and brother were all out in the fields.

The girl sat at the edge of the trees and watched. The family was not grieving. They did not pound their flesh or wail or cry. They did not lie abed for weeks on end, unwashed, uneating. There was a space, perhaps, where a seventh person may have once stood or worked or sat but…they went about their day. They went about their chores. They spoke. Sometimes they smiled.

They must have been able to see the girl from where they worked. Must have known who she was, or if they did not, wondered, but they did not come up to speak to her. They had no questions.

The girl wailed and cried. She beat her breast and when that did not give her solace, she took a sharp stone and beat with that instead. All the tears and all the pain and all the noise did not wash the grief away. The people below turned away, setting their backs to her noise and her clamour.

Icy rain folded in, slipping on shadowed feet down from frost and cliffs and pines. The girl got up. She walked into the village. Rain followed on her heels, dark, iced with the mountain. It filled the girl's hair, her clothing, her eye-lashes, her boots.

She walked into the town. She stood at the centre of the town. She screamed. She screamed and wailed and tore at her clothing. People stepped around her. The louder she became, the busier everyone seemed.

After a time, she stopped.

The girl walked away. She left the busy, unseeing town. She walked past the depleted family, blind in their busy-ness. She climbed up and up, through the rocks and the clefts, along the paths, around the lake, to her home.

There, she took a knife from the kitchen.

She sent for her mother.

•

It took her mother several days to descend. Her mother moved at her own pace, following her own cycles.

She descended late in the afternoon, heavily cloaked and robed. She took a seat opposite the girl.

"You called," the woman said.

"My silence," the girl said. "Has always screamed at you."

"I do not hear it," the mother said.

"I screamed for you," the girl said. "In the town. On the hill above that family."

"I did not hear it."

"Do you hear me now?" the girl asked.

"I am seated here," the mother said. "Right here. Where I have always been. We are conversing."

"You come down only when you have to," the girl said.

"I give you everything I have to give."

"It's not enough."

"It is more than my mother gave to me," the mother said.

The girl stood up, knife in her hand. She crossed to her mother. Her mother stood as well.

"You'd kill me?" she said. "What harm have I done you? You are my everything."

The girl reached to her mother, pulling at the sodden tie of her heavy robe. She set the knife in and cut the tie. The heavy coat dropped away. Robes beneath, soaked and ancient and knotted. The girl cut at these. Layer after layer, each heavy and wet, dropped away. The pieces fell about their feet.

"This will not work," the mother said. "These things are mine. Not yours."

"They stand between us," the girl said. "They weigh you down."

"This is not how it is done," the mother said.

"What *you* are doing is not the way of it, either."

The last piece of clothing dropped away. The girl cast the knife down upon the pile of sodden, discarded coats and clothing. Her mother…not naked. Empty. There was *nothing* under the clothing.

"This," the mother said, gesturing at the soaked, rotting robes about their feet. "This was the shape of me."

The girl stepped back. In disrobing her mother, she had somehow attained a heavy black fur coat. It was soaked. Dripping.

"The loss," the girl realised, touching the coat. "Of my mother. My responsibility in that."

The mother displayed her hands. Frail, empty hands, trembling in nothingness. Her placid, serene face, a mask in the nothing. All her heaviness and grief and the shape of her was piled and heaped about their feet, set to trip and tangle any step either of them took.

A thought occurred to the girl. She pressed a hand under her coat, fingers reaching in to find the skin of her breast, so recently beat and bruised with a rock. She could not find her breast, nor the wound, nor any flesh at all.

Beneath the sodden, heavy coat was…

"Leave, if you will," the mother said. "It walks with you. The pines and the cliffs and the frost and the rain. The salt of it."

"It's not mine," the girl said.

"I made it yours, as my mother made it mine."

Tears burned the girl's eyes. Fresh, hot salt. They burned against the cold.

"Does it free you?" the girl asked, voice choked. "Giving it to me?"

Her mother was gone.

The girl was alone. Her coat, dripping.

Flightless on the Way to the North

BY JORDAN BIANCHI

As a kit, I'd always dreamt
Of chasing northern skies;
To sail beneath the arcs of light,
That sway and mesmerize.

These dreams of light, they beaconed hope,
That greatness was for me.
They kept me fierce and full and free,
That nothing could not be.

I sew my sails, kiss kin goodbye,
And leave the land I know.
The stars, they guide me northern-bound,
And encourage me ever so.

As aurora skies are within my reach,
Storm clouds overtake my sight.
A rush of wind, cascades of snow—
My sails they rip, I fall below.

Aurora

Alone, and saddened, on an icy shore,
Ashamed and full of woe.
Reckless I had flown, and failed
To see cosmic threads sew curtains aglow.

But the villagers of this northern isle,
They listen to my heart's defeat.
Their pelts all white, their manners sweet;
They take me in and bake warm treats.

Although the sun here does not rise,
The villagers don't strain their eyes
By candlelight or lighthouses bright.
They make their own joy and dance all night.

Perhaps this land will be my home
In a burrow under mounds of snow.
But can I simply, permanently,
Forget my dreams to soar?

When the wind stirs, crisp and cool,
Creases in it speak.
It beckons me to take the chance,
To stretch my wings and leap.

The lights beyond that summon still
Are not just in the northern sky;
They mirror what is deep inside,
A part of me I'd tried to hide.

My dreams burn bright within me still,
And for that I must be strong.
My inner light was meant to soar,
To the aurora's prismatic song.

So whether we choose to take a step
And hoist ourselves into the sky,
Or rest on coastlines, tired, spent,
While ships sail by and by.

We must be gentle, not so hard,
To meet our dreams with grace.
When timing's true, storm clouds will clear,
And welcome our embrace.

Dreaming Herbs

Herbs for Lucid Dreaming

Disclaimer: Please consult your doctor before ingesting any herb you aren't familiar with. Some herbs should not be consumed while pregnant.

Tips for Lucid Dreaming:

Before using any dream herb, it's best to set an intention for your dreaming. Whether you want to connect to a deeper self, travel or to remember when you wake.

Use the herbs whichever way is best for you—smoke, infusion, tea. Create a restful environment, free from distractions. You can even pair herbs like Catnip and Mugwort for a fuller experience (consult an herbalist for the most benefit.)

When doing any kind of magick, make sure you're in a safe space, alone or with people you trust.

And last, jot down your dreams. Journaling as soon as you wake will improve dream recall and over time you'll realize patterns.

Herbs for Lucid Dreaming—this is not an exhaustive list:

Mexican Dream Herb (Calea zacatechichi):
From Mexico and Central America this herb will boost clarity and dream awareness and recall.
Use as a dry tea. It can also be smoked or even used in a dream sachet under the pillow.
Bitter.

Mugwort (Artemisia Vulgaris):
Stimulates the center of spiritual vision, enhances deep dream state, improves color and improves dream recall.
Use as a dry tea, tincture, infused in oil or burned as incense.
Bitter.

Blue Lotus (Nymphaea caerulea):
Revered in Egyptian spirituality for its euphoric, deep relaxation effects and memorable dreaming.
Use as a dry tea or infused into wine.
Earthy. Bitter. Faintly sweet.

Wild Dagga (Leonotis leonurus):
As with cannabis, this herb can elevate your mood and induce peace. It can also create mental clarity which helps with lucid dreaming.
Use as a dry tea.
Sweet with bitter edge.

German Chamomile (Matricaria chamomilla):
One of the nine sacred herbs of the Saxon people, chamomile has been used to relax the mind for vivid dreaming for centuries.
Use dried for tea or tincture drops

Valerian (Valerian Officinalis)
Praised for its comforting aspect, this herb is a muscle relaxant

and sleep aid. Promoting deep sleep and vivid dreams this herb also helps you remember when you wake.
Use as a tincture in water, tea or under your tongue.
Bitter. Earthy. Maybe spicy.

Passionflower (Passiflora Incarnata)
Commonly known as Maypop or Wild Apricot. This herb acts as a sedative and can balance energy. It reduces stress to quiet the mind for dreaming.
Use as a tea.
Herbaceous. Slightly sweet.

Yarrow (Achillea millefolium**)**
Yarrow is a medicinal herb with dreaming benefits. It works on the circulatory system to help energy flow. It strengthens our connections to dreams and helps in astral travel.
Use as a tea, tincture or flower essence.
Bitter. Astringent.

Lemon Balm (Melissa Officianalis)
A nootropic herb improving memory and cognition, it also calms and induces sleep.
Use as a tea or tincture.
Sour. Sweet. Minty.

Holy Basil (Ocimum Tenuiflorum)
Known as Tusli, this herb is said to be a "gateway" between this world and the other. Great for manifesting through dreaming
Use as a tea or tincture.
Bitter. Spicy. Astrigent. Minty.

36

Ocean Burial

BY LUCY ZHANG

When we send the dead off, we cut open their chests and remove their hearts, so the weight of their emotions may be lifted. We peel off their faces, so none may judge them by their appearances in the afterlife. We drain their brains and carve out their organs, so they are free of the stresses and hunger that plague the earth. Grandpa once performed these tedious operations, although now his hands cannot hold the scalpel without shaking like thunder, and so I have taken over most ceremonies.

"Don't cut while making that face," he tells me as I incise through the side of the corpse's cheek.

"What face?" I ask, focusing my fingers on the top of the blade and drawing one cohesive line from the edge of the ear to the cheekbone to the forehead.

"Like you'd eat their souls before they have a chance to find their way to the other realm."

I attempt to flatten the upward curves in my mouth. Grandpa has always said not to express my joy so easily since it scares the townspeople, even unnerving the old ladies who sell fish eyeballs as delicacies. I can't help it. Stifling joy doesn't come naturally to me, and emptying the bodies to set their souls free sends my hands tingling, one precise cut after another, until I've liberated not only the dead but also the body which we feed back into the earth. The earth sings its pleasures with soft winds and hollow rustling.

"And don't spend too long with the organs. They need to go into the earth while still warm," Grandpa warns as he turns to head into our small cottage. The days grow colder earlier. His knees can no longer handle the chill.

"I won't," I affirm.

I probably will.

Grandpa and I are the only few who carry out the ceremonies since no one else can stomach it. And because we're foreigners who made a home here, and what better job to toss us than the lowest paid, most unwanted. Grandpa brought me here while I was a toddler, so I remember little of life before. He refuses to tell me much about our origins—not my parents, my birth, not even the reason for my dark hair and eyes, as though someone had blotted through my pupils with endless ocean depths.

"When you're done, come in for dinner," Grandpa calls.

I smell the familiar sharp, floral scent of honeysuckle and sweet potato soup. Grandpa says this recipe comes from a place where flowers grow from boulders, their roots splitting open the rock and turning minerals to dust. Grandpa grew up eating flowers to build strength in his body. Although the flowers here can't crack open rocks, Grandpa plucks honeysuckles from trees and brews teas and soups with them as a substitute. Our bodies accumulate toxins quickly, especially away from our homeland, so he has me eating honeysuckle with every meal to cleanse. Grandpa hurries me to the table, a rock slab he smoothed and polished until it lost all its edges, and a marble could lay motionless on its surface.

"You forgot to wash up again," he lectures. "The souls will return to drag you away."

"You keep saying that, Papa, but all I see is a whole lot of nothing," I reply. "Not even the dead could make it through the water and back. The ocean is bigger than the netherworld."

"That's what it seems like to you," Grandpa says as he slops a ladle of overcooked sweet potato mush into my bowl. "But we come from across the ocean, where it's warm all year round, and you can grow fruit sweeter than the honey here."

"Seems stupid to me that you would leave," I mumble.

I know he escaped some ambiguous terror and risked his life to bring me here, where I could grow, even if nourished by a land that freezes over for half the year. Better frozen than dead, as Grandpa likes to say.

"This is a good place," he proclaims.

"You complain a lot about this place you consider good."

"Very funny." He sits on the carpet we skinned from a bear that attempted to ravage our supply of dried fish hanging across a line between two trees. He prefers to be close to the ground and rarely sits on our chairs. "There are going to be a lot more deaths now that it's getting colder. We're going to be busy for a while."

I roll up my sleeves. "I'm much faster than I was before."

"I won't be able to contribute," Grandpa says, attempting to flex his hands. His fingers refuse to budge beyond their angled, bent state, perpetually in the position of a claw. "So our count this year will probably end up the same as the previous year."

I frown. "So we still won't be able to afford a boat?"

"We're getting there. Don't worry about the money. If we can't buy a boat, I'll teach you to build one."

Grandpa used to build everything with his two hands. He carved my comb from a tree branch and engraved it with swirling clouds and lotus flowers. He didn't trust what store vendors sold at their stalls, although now that we have no alternative since his hands have stiffened, he goes from stall to stall lecturing the craftsmen for their shortcomings until he finally settles on the cheapest products.

"And this boat will be able to take us all the way across the sea?" I ask, skeptical.

"There and back and many more journeys. Not that such will be necessary. We only need one homecoming."

"How do you know home will still be as you remember?"

"We come from a place that resists change. Even time is held constant for certain parts of the year in which no creatures age, and we go without nights for days."

"That doesn't mean it hasn't changed. Hasn't it been forever since you were last home?" I argue.

"When you are old, you will do anything for the safety of family," he continues, ignoring my question. "No sacrifice is too little."

Grandpa is full of contradictions: one day he'll be telling me about the horrors he fled to take me here, another day he'll be wistful and romanticize even the least pleasant of details like the types of parasites that resided in his hometown.

"Maybe the souls we send off have gone there first," I muse.

Grandpa snorts. "There's no way the dead can make it that far."

"Even without their faces and hearts? I thought that'd make them light enough to go anywhere."

"Anywhere into the heavens. It's different here, tethered to the ground."

I take my bowl to the door and slip on thick, tall boots. I wash the dishes by the river whose water flows strongly enough we hardly ever need to scrub. Grandpa continues to sit and stare at the empty wall, either lost in a trance or having fallen asleep with his eyes open again. I keep telling him he strains his body too much at this age, but all he does is chug a cup of boiled cordyceps water and call his body as good as new.

I tighten the latches on the windows, so the wind can't rattle them against their frames. Slowly and quietly, so Grandpa doesn't wake.

•

The monsters eat through the center of the town before they come to us.

Moments before they arrive, the clatter of wheels on the streets and sharp pitter-patters of bamboo sandals against the ground halt. Even the caws of crows who like to swoop down for discarded mantou and fish eyeballs vanish.

I remain focused on the clean whoosh of my scalpel as I sharpen it against a stone. I am preparing to operate on a boy's body sent to us by parents who could only pay in baskets of gooseberries. Grandpa never rejects any clients. I don't think he understands how money works.

We first hear a soft scraping at the door—short sounds you could mistake for knocking. I peek through the eye hole and see stray leaves on the ground and long, stringy shadows cast on the base of the door—the limbs of the willow tree that threaten to overtake our home.

"Don't open the door," Grandpa warns as I place my hand on the door handle. He stands behind me, holding a kitchen knife and a pan. I take a step back, and let him scope out the entrance. He leans his weight on the door as he strains his neck forward and clicks his tongue.

"If you don't leave the house, you'll be safe. But as soon as you step outside, you've entered its domain," he says.

"What about our work?" I ask. "How will we ever leave this town if we can't even leave our house?"

"We simply need to wait," Grandpa answers. "There will be a time when we can return home. If you are patient." Then he fastens the bolt on the lock and drags over a rock to block the door.

I dislike leaving a job unfinished, a soul half tethered and half drifting away because I haven't yet extracted their innards. The boy I am working on is younger than me. He has beautiful, glassy eyes and a ribcage so stiff I had to cleave it open to remove the heart. His body rests in the shed across our house. I can't remember if I locked it, and fear the lurking monster might eat the boy's final chance of departure. Thus, while Grandpa sleeps, I remove the stone, unfasten the bolt, and creep outside. A man-eating beast won't want me, I reason. My flesh likely tastes sour and putrid because of all the fish I catch from the coast and eat without cooking properly.

"I mean no harm I mean no harm," I whisper as I walk toward the shed, scanning side to side for any monsters. Only empty fields and swaying trees.

The boy's body rests on the table in good condition, as though sleeping from a long night. Of course, his eye sockets have been hollowed out, and his ears cut off so he is more like a rock gnome with their flat, smooth heads punctured with holes for eyes and mouths. I begin to cut away at his chest, removing his stomach and liver and intestine. If you eat before crossing into the afterlife, the extra weight might drown you in the ocean. I finish before dusk, and send the boy off.

•

"There are no monsters," I tell Grandpa confidently.

"There are," he refutes, pointing to the window where even from here, we can usually see the faint silhouettes of people out and about. Instead, there is no one. "Else where would a whole town of people have gone? Eaten, I tell you."

"But we're fine."

"Only for so long. They are coming. You can hear it in the air: the quiet, the death of free movement."

"What's coming for us?" I ask again. Every time, Grandpa refuses to answer.

"They've crossed the ocean. Followed us here," he

murmurs. Then he looks up at me, rising to a stand as he leans his weight on the wall. "We will leave. It's about time anyway."

"Where are we going? We don't have a boat to cross the waters, nor a cart or horse to pull us deeper inland," I argue.

Grandpa waves his hand at me and begins placing the small trinkets he carried from his hometown in a bag. "Start packing. We'll leave as soon as we're done."

"We'll never be done," I whisper.

Grandpa has misplaced half his things. It'll take at least a week for him to serendipitously stumble upon them and safely place them in a sack. Still, I pocket my best scalpel into my deep, inner pocket, and sew it shut.

That night, I sneak away to the town center. Although the quiet descends upon our home like a fog, I haven't seen a single dead soul make its way to our ceremonial grounds. Even souls who haven't had their faces and hearts removed gravitate here, clinging to the ground and dragging themselves against the rocks and sand while their bodies weigh themselves down. Grandpa used to perform free ceremonies on these souls, but now that I'm the only one physically capable of performing the cuts, I only operate on those who can pay. There are already too many dead, and Grandpa thinks we've saved more money than in reality.

Corn fields surround the road to town, some patches of earth razed to the ground with heaps of dry, ashy remnants of stalks. Other patches contain corn that has yet to ripen, although even when ripe, the corn is too tough to eat so it gets fed to the pigs. I cut across the fields, dodging severed stalks that protrude from the ground like sharpened knives. In the mornings, the elderly will cull the stalks and work the fields with their hunched backs and large, bamboo hats that cover their entire faces in shadow. I've never passed through in the evening though. Grandpa wouldn't let me—he claimed it was unsafe, especially since the townspeople whisper behind our backs, fearful of how Grandpa arrived from cursed lands overseas.

"Fear drives the most terrifying behavior, always stay home at night," he'd say.

But I can't blame the townspeople. Grandpa has always been off putting, and if I had been born here, I'd think of him as weird too. Whenever we went into town together for salt and sugar and another armful sized jar of fermented beancurd, he'd drape five necklaces of green jade over each of our necks and dress us in loose, long fitting dresses that sweep the ground, as though we were ghosts drifting through. When he haggled with the shopkeepers, he'd speak to them in soft tones and stare at them with a sharp gaze as though hypnotizing a snake. We'd leave with full bags at less than half the market price, swindling them out of a profit. As a result, people have tried to avoid selling things to us altogether. Most of all, Grandpa doesn't worship their god even after I asked him to go along with their rituals, so they wouldn't cut us off from water.

"If you give up your ideals, you become nothing," he claimed.

If you die from thirst, you also become nothing. But Grandpa knows more about death than I do, so I refrain from arguing further.

The corn fields lead to the center of town where dirt melds into rock and buildings stand in disorganized rows, each fenced in and surrounded by a coop of chicken or barrels full of corn. Even in the marketplace, where at its quietest, widows wheel around their carts selling blocks of beancurd and dragon floss candies to late night snackers, I find no one. As I near the school, I shimmy through the two stones marking the entrance. I follow the walls until I reach a window whose curtains are pulled aside, the view inside unfettered and clear. I rub my breaths' fog that creeps over the window and squint.

What I originally thought to be a dark room is instead a moving, black mist. It circulates the room, touching every corner, neither resting nor accelerating. I knock on the window. The mist's movements stutter and spin toward my direction.

The closer it gets, the more I can make out bone-like structures crawling from behind the cloaked blackness, like thousands of spider legs shuffling and crackling, a sound audible even from behind the wall. They appear connected by a central spine that worms its way around. Although its full length is unclear, the bone structures emerge from all sides of the room, the creature layered and barely contained in the small space.

This must be the monster Grandpa was talking about, although it seems far less scary than other creatures we'd encountered. The red wolves who gnawed off the tip of my thumb, though thankfully they'd dropped the digit and Grandpa was able to reattach it to my hand. The white snake that lulled me into the ocean before I learned how to swim. Monsters are attracted to us because we deal with death, and they originate from beyond the boundary at which we dance and linger, guardians of entry and exit.

I push open the window. The black mist jolts. The bone structures move like a tidal wave, spilling down the ceiling and wrenching themselves through the gap. The light taps of their legs on the surface accumulate into a chorus of clicking. I cover my ears, but it still sounds as though even my bones are rattling. The monster slows and spreads with each movement. As it passes me, I notice that each bone piece is a different size and color, some thin and smooth like fingers of the young, others coarse and yellowed like toes of the old. As it winds around the school building, I pinch my thigh to get my legs to run. I don't look back to see if it follows.

I stomp over the severed corn stalks, their edges poking into my feet. It only somewhat hurts as my feet don't linger on any one surface for long. By the time I arrive back, Grandpa is standing outside, hands on his hips, lips pursed, eyebrows drawn downward in straight, ferocious slants. His knapsack loops around his frail shoulders, sagging behind his back as though full of stones.

"We must leave. Now." Grandpa says nothing of how I

disobeyed orders. "Its traces are on you. It will be here soon once it finishes devouring the town."

"We haven't packed our tools," I protest and point to the shed where many of our shears and saws and skin graft knives hang.

"You can buy those anywhere, and if you really have to, you can perform a ceremony with a single scalpel," Grandpa replies as he begins to walk, passing me and ignoring my torn shoes. "Let's go. There isn't much time until the monsters catch up to us."

I follow behind him, constantly turning my head to look back. It takes a long time for us to walk out of view of the house.

"What if we cohabitate with the monsters?" I suggest. "They clearly haven't done us any harm despite devouring the remainder of the town."

Grandpa shakes his head. "These creatures will turn on you the moment they grow hungry and discover you're the only few left. Just because you can send human souls into the afterlife doesn't mean you can control a monster."

"You don't know that," I protest.

We have nearly crossed the remains of the cornfields and are beginning to enter the mountain ranges. Few people venture here since the rocky, sharp terrain has catapulted a number of people to their deaths, and the cool, dry air feels like it'd scrape off your cheeks. Grandpa marches ahead, as though he knows what exists beyond the summit, further and further from the home he came from.

"I know it. I know it well," he repeats. We climb in zig zags, gaining elevation and dodging thorny bushes. Grandpa turns around and points to the town we can see from here. The monster subsumes the buildings, and I briefly identify a few corners of roofs and the center fountain before the black mist washes over them. "It's a Swallowing. That's how your birthplace vanished overnight. How they were all absorbed—

body and soul and all."

"Aren't we supposed to be crossing the ocean to go home? That's what we've been saving all this money for. How can we return to…" I pause. "A Swallowing?"

"The ocean is not safe if the monster has even crossed those lengths. It must've followed us over, biding its time."

I pant. Even though Grandpa's flat feet hurt his back with each step, and his head bobs like an unstable ball balancing on a pebble, he charges up the mountain with a ferocity I hadn't seen in him since his final ceremony performed on a mother and unborn daughter.

"But we can't run forever. We'll run out of places. Can't we tell the monster to stop following us? Or send it back to the afterlife?"

"We will leave. The world is big. There will always be somewhere to go," Grandpa replies firmly. He stumbles on a boulder loosely held by the dirt. I hold his arm and snap off a tree branch for him to use as a cane.

"I don't think we are hiking fast enough to evade it." I observe.

Grandpa shakes his head. "The Swallowing is a slow process. We will be good for another few years before it comes after us."

"But why is it coming after us? Can't it go back to where it came, or follow someone else?"

"Most humans only skim the surface of death," he says. "But we wrench it apart and starve the in-between worlds of both souls or corpses. This job and power don't come without a price. The monster is our natural enemy. We starved them into existence."

I refrain from suggesting that we stop performing ceremonies. Even I know the proposal sounds ridiculous. Just as we eat and sleep and breathe, we send the dead to rest to ease the tightness within our heads, a pressure that accumulates overtime until our skulls threaten to burst. Grandpa says this pain pervades our lineage—how it drives us to fulfill our duties as guardians and messengers. I care little about the pain. I enjoy watching the lightness of a soul drift beyond the horizon, as though a tiny part of me joins them on a journey, free to roam as far as the afterlife extends.

"What if we fight back somehow? Surely there's a way to defeat such a monster. Nothing is infallible," I suggest.

Grandpa thwacks one of the boulders with the makeshift cane I handed him. It shakes under his light force, so he walks around it, forcing his legs through a thin pathway between rock and tree trunk. I take a large step upward onto the loose boulder, waiting for its quaking to settle before jumping off and landing in a squat.

"No fighting. We can only evade it until our bodies lose their energy and force." Grandpa must notice the frustration mounting in my face, and I immediately try to loosen my frown and rub my temples. Grandpa likes to joke that I wear my emotions like a sheer scarf left to blow in everyone's faces. "This is a cycle of life. Something must carry us away in the end, and we cannot send off each other," he adds.

"Why not?" I look away to conceal my glare. Grandpa answers questions on a whim, I swear.

"Too emotional. Can you promise that you'd peel off my face, cut out my heart, empty my body? It is a better fate for a creature to take us whole than leave pieces of us behind, scattered and incomplete."

I charge ahead to scope out the area and choose a viable path that cuts through the forest and winds around a stream of water too rapid for Grandpa to maintain his balance. After finding a shaded area where a cluster of leaves have fallen into a cushioned pile, I wait for him. The top of his head makes it into my view first. Then his face, neck, and arms swaying back and forth with the cane, neither rushed nor hurried, steady like a turtle.

"So we're not running away." I wish to confirm.

"We are creating new homes and bridges to the afterlife, that is all." As Grandpa makes his way to my side, he points into the open air in front of us. "Look."

I follow his gaze and finger. I see clusters of trees so dense they cover my view of the dirt, canopies so full of layered greens, I'm not sure where the sun gives life to the ground. I guess this is something you simply have to trust. Life doesn't spring from nowhere.

Don't Wake up Too Fast

BY JON NEGRONI

In the month they call the Dreaming Cold, when the sea hisses louder and the wind pushes forth a rusted sugarcane chill, Abuela Mima stopped speaking in her sleep. She could always whisper to the dead when she felt like it. I saw her do it firsthand for years. In the act, her body goes stiff as driftwood, her eyes fluttering, and out comes names only our elders remember…Antuca, Calderín, the girl with the gored belly from the hurricane of '32.

But this year, Mima's mouth stays sealed. No mutters or groans or even smoke from the oil lamp to beget listening ears. The house feels wrongly quiet, in fact, as if something thick and wet were clogging the throat of the place. I can't let Mima pass on without asking her a very important question about myself. And so I do what I'm not supposed to do. I go looking for her dreams.

•

In my family, we pass down instructions for dreamwalking like others pass down recipes for coquito, the holiday rum drink I've indulged in since I was eleven. To make dreamwalking happen, you grind up the nightshade from the cliffs of Cabo Rojo. You mix it with honey left three nights under a new moon. You fast until your stomach aches a name back to you. Then you take the name like a key and slide it into the lock of another world.

I am seventeen. The last girl in the family line. My mother says our kind of magic doesn't work when the Wi-Fi's strong. But when the mango trees go naked and the frogs stop singing, everything becomes more possible than usual. The deepest mystical everything. It shows up in the silence after the holiday celebrations. It's as subtle as an elder who stops in the middle of a story because they forgot the ending.

The old roads in my head reopen. That's how I find myself kneeling in the dark on Mima's tiled floor, maybe minutes from her death, lighting a candle with three wicks, wearing her nightgown like it's Halloween on Christmas.

I whisper her name three times, not loud enough to wake her but loud enough for the other…thing to hear. And then I go under.

The tile melts. The night bends. I drop through the floor and into the hush that waits between sleep and whatever feels alive. There are no colors here if you squint. Only glimmering fish scales and tears lit by candlelight. The salty space has a waxy thin layer of hibiscus, only turned rotten. Oh, I know this place. We call it *el umbral*. The threshold.

I land on my feet inside the old courtyard in Ciales, the one we burned down before María flooded our hopes. The mango tree stands whole again, heavy with fruit too ripe to touch. Somewhere, a rooster screams like a security alarm. I feel for the amulet around my neck—una semilla de guanábana—painted black and passed down by women who didn't live long enough to tell me why it exists or even why I need it.

"Abuela?" I call out, but nothing echoes. So frustrating. It really is a dream. Nothing I want quite works how it should.

Instead, the door to the old kitchen swings open and something steps out wearing Mima's face. Certainly not the Mima I know, the one who spits tamarind seeds out the side of her mouth like no one else can see her do it. This is her younger, bonier self with cheeks like crushed shells. She's wearing a red slip and no shoes, and her eyes glow like blown glass in a kiln.

"Nene, dios mío, you shouldn't be here," she says. "Qué Chavienda."

"I know, I know. But I came to find you."

"I know your mother didn't say you could come."

"She can't do this anymore. Or I guess she doesn't want to."

Mima looks at me the way abuelas do when they know you've been kissing the neighbor boy and lying about it. Then she lifts one arm and points. Not at me, but behind me. I turn.

There's a second me standing there. Eyes wide, mouth slack, dressed in my uniform from San Juan Catholic, knees bruised from chasing girls up and down the knolls. My dream-double's holding a match between her fingers. It burns steady, never dwindling. I turn back to Mima.

"Well, don't just stand there," Mima says, hands on hips. "Ask whatever it is you came to ask."

I tilt my head, unsure.

Mima shakes her head. "Did you really do nothing to prepare before you decided to invade my sleep? Dios mío, nene, too much like your mother."

My mouth opens, but nothing makes itself heard. I realize I don't really have a question, let alone a plan. I think of my real Mima, slack-jawed and still. I think of my mother's hands scrubbing bleach into tile grout while crying over a voicemail. I think of the way the winter island rain doesn't fall anymore. It only seeps into the ground and vanishes without evidence it ever existed.

It ever existed. "Abuela, I have a question. About me. Or the family in general. About the…dreams. Do we hear the same voice whispering names of the dead?"

I struggle to get the words out, but out they come. I want to feel relief when Mima is about to answer, but as I look upon her face, my double emerges from behind her, as if she'd been living in Mima's shadow. The double smiles with wicked teeth, and the courtyard begins to burn all around me. The mangoes blister as the singular flame eats inward, not outward, as if the fire had been loitering beneath the stones. Smoke drowns the double's knees but doesn't touch her. She stands calm, the match still burning untouched to her skin.

I don't move, same goes for Mima. This is the way of dreamwork. Running is the last thing you do in a place like this.

"You're hearing voices?" Mima asks, her voice more brittle now.

"I don't know, maybe."

She tuts, a sound that comes from someplace familiar. Mom, probably. "Don't lie to your abuela, especially not here. You'll leave a stain in the threshold."

The other me steps forward. Her clean hands and dry eyes are the most unique "this is definitely not me" things about her. Also, the match is still holding its shape. Something tells me she wants to drop it at my feet.

"I think…" I swallow, trying to ignore the double now pacing around us like an indifferent shark. "I think I dreamed your death before it happened. Before the real you outside of this dream stopped speaking."

Mima cocks her head. It's the exact gesture I make when I'm trying not to cry on the phone. When I'm holding the sound in the back of my throat, pretending it's a cough.

"Tell me what happened in this supposed dream of yours," she says.

"I told you I don't remember."

"Nene, tell me anyway. Put some work into it, we're running out of time."

Annoyed, I close my eyes. Partly to get her gaze off me. The dream…there was a hallway, narrow as a spine. Doors on either side, but they opened onto mirrors instead of rooms. My reflection kept changing—child, woman, crone, back again. At the end of the hall was a window that didn't show the sky. Only a mound of red earth and Mima's sandals sticking out. I couldn't move or make a sound even though I desperately wanted to scream.

When I open my eyes, Mima is gone, and the double is right in front of me. We are the same height. The same scar under the chin, from the bike crash in Santurce. She leans in, presses the burning match to my collarbone.

It doesn't hurt, though. I inhale through my teeth, and the courtyard vanishes.

I expect to wake up, but I end up falling again. Not far, thankfully, but hard. Dreams don't usually hurt, and a fall like this should probably kill me enough to wake me. Instead I feel a smattering ringing, like sound itself is hurting me as I land in water up to my knees. The water is still, warm, brackish. It reaches up my gown and settles there.

Around me, a mangrove forest breathes in the dark. The trees lean toward me, their roots hunched like ribs. I smell blood and coconut and fermented algae.

I hear only my own breath as I feel my collarbone where the match burned me. Like she branded me with something beneath my skin.

From the water, voices rise into flittering arguments, at least that's my guess. The language isn't English or Spanish. It's what I imagine the trees say to each other when people aren't around. Weirdly, I sort of understand it. Like I can feel the meaning of each word, more or less.

You were not meant to dreamwalk alone.

You seek what was already given.

You are your own question.

Great, even in a forgotten spiritual language, nothing in el umbral makes sense. I take another step. The water deepens. My gown pulls like a tongue at my hips.

"Fine, I'll bite. What do you mean I seek what's already given? Abuela Mima didn't tell me anything. She stopped speaking."

The mangroves shake, though there's no breeze pulling at them. Something peeks out from the water ahead of me. A figure…slight, back turned, hair plaited thick down her spine. A white dress floats around her like the earliest morning mist, painted a faded moonlight.

I try to figure out if I know her. Definitely not the younger Mima or my double. Not my own mother, not with a smile like that. Maybe…the stranger from my dream? The one I saw in the mirror when I was the crone. She's far older than any of us, and maybe that makes her me in a sense. A future me I hadn't dared imagine. Wrinkled hands. Necklaces of teeth and glass. A mouth that knows silence.

"You can't save Mima," she says. "She gave up her words to buy you some time."

"Wait, what?" My hands close into fists. "The hell are you talking about?"

"You heard the voice, which means it's your time."

My throat tightens. "For crying out loud, can you talk like a person? Mima's dying!"

"She's crossing into something new, and the problem is that it's too early for her. She's doing it so you don't have to. Now you must take her place."

I want to scream at her or maybe run away until this stupid dream ends. But my mind pushes me to think about what this future me is really saying.

Mima dreamwalked first. She saw me die, didn't she? She was about to say my name when she whispered to the dead, so instead…she stopped speaking.

I stare at the woman—at myself, or the version of myself I could become. Her eyes don't blink. They've probably seen too much for blinking.

"She crossed early," I say aloud. "So I wouldn't."

She nods out of something heavier and more embarrassing than pity.

"It's no gift," she says. "It's an exchange. Her voice for your life. Her dreams for your delay. But you must accept it. You must be willing."

Sick. Disgusting. I have to accept Mima dying on my behalf? No. I instantly refuse. I'd rather dreamwalk as a corpse for the rest of my days, never to wake up. I could never do something like that.

"You have to," a voice says from nowhere. It almost sounds

like Mima. "You're the last of the family line. Don't be selfish."

"I don't care!" I shout into nothing. The future me vanishes. I sink further into the water. It presses cold against my ribs now. How could Mima make me do something like this? Let her throw life away like it's nothing? Who would do something like that?

The mangroves stop breathing. The water stills. I feel the brand on my collarbone pulse. Not painfully, but firmly. Like a heartbeat inside the skin. Behind me, I hear the faintest sound: Mima humming. An old lullaby with no words. The one I used to pretend I didn't like.

And just like that, I know what I have to do. I kneel into the water. Let it take the rest of my weight. I whisper my full name, a name of the dead, into the earth beneath it.

I promise the forest I will learn the old languages properly next time. I promise to ask the dead for names I don't yet know I've forgotten. I promise to remember everything and everyone and anyone.

I wake up on the tile.

The candle is burned down to the wick. The room smells like honey, now, though I've no idea why or how. My hands tremble, my chest still feels like it should be wet.

Beside me, Mima exhales. Her fingers twitch once, twice, and settle. She doesn't say anything, but I hear words, anyway.

Don't wake up too fast.

Half asleep, I lean
over the edge of our arctic pond,
a chamber of stored winters, silent
and cold as ancestral breath held too long.

Ear pressed to its chilled skin,
I hear no word, only the slow churning
of frozen current-clouds, older than language.
Beneath the surface,
chromosomes thrum like taut, icy wires,
chilled harp strings still stringing
by unseen hands.

Underfoot—ankles, wrists, vertebrae—
a thaw breathes across
the water's rigid mirror-face.
I feel its vapor swell, like a spell,
emanate through the lineage-braid,
then stir an earthly warmth
upward in me.

Aurora

Ripples release, swim as if
they knew their role,
forming a whirlpool.
I recognize the echoes of an ancient cycle.

Not a message, but a rhythm.
Not an answer, but a remembering.
I don't walk forward.

In the midst
of this solstice grip, ice decides
to swing wide, into a snow-veil
and a path appears—loops back, bone-bright—
as if a dream-light were here
spiraling my spine;
as if my being and time were etched
in the curl of a ring,
not the arrow of a line.

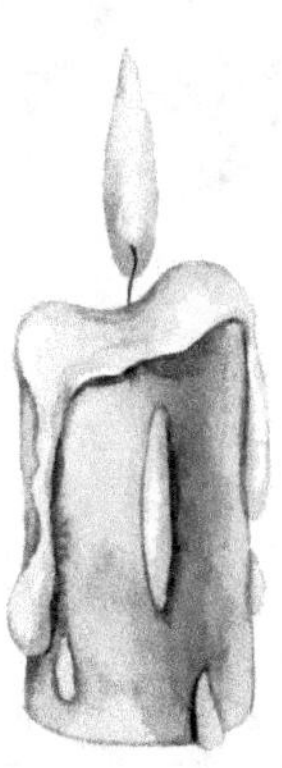

A Winter like We Dreamt Before

BY JM CYRUS

"Finna?"

His voice is exactly how she remembered. Husky and low, the sound tasting like turmeric and dark red. Finna hopes she heard pleasure in the tone. She knows not to hope for joy. But all she's sure she heard was surprised politeness.

She doesn't look away from his face. She notes the mouth in a line, the jaw tense at the joints, the eyes ever so slightly narrowed. She sees nothing that gives her hope. *But*, she tells herself, *there's nothing to make me lose hope either.*

He looks the same. Ageless. Though there's something different. His face had always seemed to hold all other ages, like a bundle of gauzes in many muted shades. But now, the layers are reordered. A faint wisp of older now sits at the surface, a man closer to fifty than twenty.

Fires above, he's still so handsome it hurts.

She notices new tattoos across his collarbone. His braids are now below his shoulders rather than to his chin. There are new gems too, nestling at the ends of each braid, stars in a night sky.

Before she can stop herself, she thinks of her differences. *Why, stupid woman, why think of your age now?* In the seventeen years since she last saw him, it didn't occur to her to worry about how she would have changed. Or maybe she ignored it. But now, the knowledge she's older coats her in a dress made of something sagging and sloppy.

She forgets how hard it's been to get here. She forgets how much she's learnt and gained and how much she has lost. Instead, all she thinks is how beautiful he still is and how ripe she has become. The freckles on what used to be blemish-free skin itch, the sprinkle of white hairs she tried to hide within her pins feel hot as a filament, and the shape of her body beneath the flatteringly draped suit feels so obvious she may as well be wearing a translucent shift.

But she holds her chin high. Her training holds, and she looks him in the eye and answers.

"Yes, Hewn, it's me."

•

The winter Finna met Hewn lived on in all her senses. She'd gone to sleep in the room with her sisters, bundled away from that winter's first dancing cold night, and looked forward to where her dreams might take her.

She'd been able to lucid dream since she was a child. When she was five, her parents realised she didn't dream like their other children nor anyone they knew. She spoke of friends and choices as if they were real to her. Where her siblings would suffer nightmares for weeks from their paternal grandmother's ghost stories, Finna asked why they didn't just change dreams instead.

Their grandmother had been only slightly offended. She was proud of her ghost stories. For a child to not be affected was adjacent to an insult.

Finna spent her childhood exploring, her imagination bridging the gap between play and dream, between day and night. Her teens dissolved into desires and impulses, the day that connected each night of fulfilled wishes slowed to a plod of responsibility, propriety and boredom.

Come young adulthood, attempts at learning a craft fell away, apprenticeships and lessons disappearing into her lust for sleep. Her parents looked at their other children, their range of trades and skills and lives—chef, blacksmith, farmer, teacher, parent—and then at Finna, who couldn't darn a sock without losing herself in daydreams. Is it any surprise that someone with a universe of possibilities beyond her closed eyes would be aimless in the day?

Finna would long for the places she could go, parties, skies, and friends she made every night. She flew amongst golden-frothed waves, explored landscapes of clouds, wore precious gems and danced in clothes of flower petals. Sounds and smells and tastes would overlap and interweave, vastly superior to the rules and clocks and demarcations of the waking world. She loved and lost and laughed and feasted and cried in her nights, and she wouldn't have it any other way. Even when her mother whispered to her about the Dream Wanderer Guild in the capital—learning of them from a travelling merchant—Finna ignored her, turning inwards and waiting for sleep.

The constraints of the waking world were difficult, dowdy, dull to twenty-year-old Finna. Though she had to be repeatedly told the names of the three towns closest to her own and the birthdays of her siblings, she knew the exact texture of the liminal space between sleeping and dreaming lay somewhere between a rose and a camellia petal. She knew to launch into dream between the quicken and the plummet when falling into sleep. She had to hold the reins of oblivion white-knuckle tight to go precisely where she wanted.

And so, on that night that she went to bed in the depths of winter, the bed a warm nest from the first proper snowstorm of the season, she let herself drift. She was ready for sandy beaches, mirror-gilded parties, and flower-encrusted lakes.

Instead, it was a land of snow.

The air smelled of salt and frost. The light, a dark-blue twilight that made her surroundings even colder. Finna looked at a world of white, the horizon hidden by the gently falling snow and tall, evergreen trees garlanded in snowfall. It looked just like a deep winter day at home.

Annoyance nipped at her. She'd left one winter for another? She tried to reroute the dream, but the reins were slippery. She knew better than to get angry. Dreams often had their own logic and time, even with her control. Perhaps there would be something wondrous here in the meantime? She picked a direction and walked.

The snow crunched beneath her feet, a feathery powder under a gentle crust. Images danced within the tree bark, they could have been engravings. Or maybe it was just the way the bark grew.

She experimented with her control, manipulating the swirling snow into dancing figures and her clothes into furs, lace, flowers. Her senses began to overlap, the squeak of the snow tasting of turquoise and middle C. She hummed and danced as she walked.

When she came upon him, she was unprepared.

She rounded a tree, and there he was. The first thing she noticed was how real the gaze from his dark eyes seemed. The second was how much she wanted him. He was stripped to the waist, revealing dark brown skin covered in looping, swirling black tattoos of hollow ferns that glittered in the half-light. And the third thing was delight at how he looked her up and down with a small smile. She blushed even in the cool snow.

Though she would try to remember how they started speaking, she could never place it. There must have been a hesitant hello between the silence and knowing how warm Hewn's hands were and how he understood her and how beautifully he kissed her. She could remember that he had four moles on his right hand and the sickle-shaped scar on his left.

She could remember how her name sounded through his lips, like dark purple and cardamom, and she remembered almost every time he told her he loved her, the way his smile leaned ever so slightly to the left, and the way he smelled of pine and emerald green, but she never remembered the first thing he said to her, no matter how she tried.

•

Finna clenches her fists. Her official suit feels too bright here in the white snow, its wool too stiff, the badges on her lapel too gaudy. Hewn stares, but she refuses to change her clothes. This is who she is now.

Her nails have left reassuringly solid, stinging half-moons in her palms. She clenches her fists again. He says nothing. The sound of her shifting feet becomes lemon and sea-green as her senses begin to jumble. *This overlap will never be boring, ever.*

Was this why Hewn lived in her memories for so long? Of course, a kiss would be unforgettable if its taste was the dusky purple of a winter dawn and the sound of a starling chorus. And if the sound of his hands as they moved over her skin was salt and honey and toasted oats and the shade between peach and apricot.

But no. It's that a single winter with Hewn meant more than any other, dream or real. Especially real.

The wind whistles dark grey. She wonders how long it's been for him. Time always passed strangely here. Curling up with each other every night all those winters ago had been eternities on their own.

Neither speaks. Anger flashes inside her for being rendered speechless. She doesn't remember the speech she's been preparing and rehearsing for as long as she's been trying to return.

He turns to face her straight rather than twisted three-quarters. His chest tattoos are different, as if the ferns have matured. He clears his throat, the sound a faint smell of ginger, but still doesn't talk. He flicks the pad of his thumb with his index fingernail. Finna realises something that gives her hope.

He's as nervous as she is.

•

Finna and Hewn's winter rendered Finna even more useless in her waking hours. After she had tried to make tea unsuccessfully for the third time that morning—once without heating the water, another without adding tea leaves, and finally leaving it to steep beyond bitterness to become dye—her father merely told her to sit to one side.

Her mother sighed. Finna noticed her mother's frustration from a distance. She knew she should be better as one knows the sky is blue. But today was cloudy, so the knowledge could be ignored. She counted the minutes until she could sleep again, see Hewn again.

Every night passed too quickly. He'd smile like a sunbeam when he saw her, lifting her by her waist and spinning her in the powdery snow, their laughter mixing like ink. His touch would make her feel more solid than she'd felt all day.

He would take her hands and kiss her palms. He would sigh into her hair about how much he missed her and what they could do tonight—walks and hunts and herb-finding and markets. His world's perpetual winter had so much to offer.

They'd exist in the snow and ice. Their breaths would ringlet together, and she wouldn't feel the cold. Instead, she felt braced, replenished, like every caress of air was stripping away something useless.

They talked of everything. There always seemed more to say and more to know. Finna wanted all of it.

She told him how much she hated her days. How a future in a small town corseted by time made her want to scream. How she'd do anything to sleep forever.

"You must live, Finna," he said, in a tone she wished were gentler but knew she deserved. "You're wasting your life if you only do something with half of it."

She ignored her anger at him. She didn't want to think about how she knew he was right.

When morning came, she woke in the room with her sisters, the fire as embers, the body heat and furs making the room constrict, and she watched her breath mist before her for one, two, three breaths and then no more.

•

"You came back," he says, the quiet breaking like a cold crust.

Finna rifles through his tone to find any hint he's glad or annoyed, but again, finds nothing but politeness.

"I had to," she answers. *Let him worry about whether it was for him or some other instruction.*

He frowns, and she hates how all her planning for how she would behave has dissolved. *Why am I behaving like this? Why can't I tell him I wanted to?*

•

The difference in their opinions on how Finna should spend her days became a boil they avoided pressing, until more than two-thirds through winter, it overtook them both.

"You have a whole life you're not using," Hewn said. "You can't just count the minutes until you sleep."

Couldn't he see things made more sense to her here? She didn't feel as real there as she did here, regardless of whether this was the dream and the other reality.

She bristled. Did he want less of her? Was she not enough for him, was that it?

Finna didn't say she'd been considering going to the healer for a drug to make her sleep for longer.

But what had started as reassurances from her whenever he brought this up—*you're all I need, I do enough, I'm here now*—shifted to more defensive—*why do you keep telling me? What I do with my day isn't your domain*—and then frustrated—*don't you trust me?*—

until finally they fought.

She was a cornered animal threatened with a cage. She said many things she didn't mean, and when she would remember it later, she hoped he hadn't either.

He told her she was running away from her responsibilities. She told him he was just like her parents. He told her that her behaviour stank of immaturity. She told him he was controlling and cruel. He told her she was pretending a life rather than living one. She said she should have known better. He said so should he.

She summoned the end of the dream with messy, uncontrolled power, treating it like slamming a door. She woke gasping and snarling into the middle of the night. After a few hours of intense stewing, she tried to get back. She wouldn't be able to remember whether it was because she wanted to continue to argue or whether she wanted to make amends.

She could not return.

Initially, she was somewhere between pleasure and righteous anger. Why would she want to go back anyway? He deserved to wait and regret. She turned her back and spent a few days in comfort, relishing the white sands of her new dreams, auburn drinks and supple bodies.

The grief caught her by surprise. Her mind re-tuned their final argument, time's lenses making her hear what he'd been really saying. He'd wanted the best for her. He hadn't been telling her to go. And yet, here she was, unable to get back.

She tried to get back, and when she arrived at the turquoise lake, the one with small boats and brass music, she wept.

She tried again and again. Her trips were chaotic, multi-colour sensory tangles, like flipping through a multi-dimensional atlas. But none of them were his. Try as she might—and how she tried!—she couldn't get back to that winter.

•

"How are you here?" he asks. *There*, she thinks, the tiniest flick beneath the politeness. *Was that hurt? Or something else? Annoyance?*

Anger?

"The same way as before," she answers, and regrets her tone again. She wasn't expecting to feel this way. She was here, and a part of her wanted to finish their fight.

"I see," he answers. He looks away and makes to turn. To leave this conversation behind. To go back to his life without her in it.

•

Her memories of their fight mutated. She replayed what she'd said to him. She had accused him of not loving her. She had told him he wanted to be rid of her. She'd called him unfeeling, false, unreal.

She veered from thinking he got what he wanted and deserved it, to thinking she was indeed a petulant child, to that she should have been kinder or meaner or angrier or more apologetic.

And then this mess, this knotted ball of argument and insecurity and fury and grief and heartbreak melted together and became something else.

It became ambition.

•

He has turned his back now to her. Finna is aware of the cold and yet her insides are filled with a sour heat. Now she remembers everything she did to get here, and it's like the years since she last saw him ruffled their feathers and faced her. "Was this how you wanted it to end? After everything?" they ask her, flaunting their time.

"Wait—" she says, the stroppiness burning away. She lets the covers fall from her voice, like armour from a naked form, revealing something soft and cool. Her voice sounds like the smell of a just-unshelled almond.

He turns back.

•

The only way Finna could calm her mind was in the chores her parents had almost given up asking her to do.

Spring was dressing everyone in pale green. Blossom and new grass filled her nose as she joined the work. Small tasks at first, making the tea, making the beds, washing the breakfast bowls. Her parents exchanged glances and held their tongues.

But before long, she was cleaning the house, the shed, the windows, the steps, doing the laundry, weeding the new growth, planting the bulbs and first potatoes.

"Who lit a fire under you?" her father said with a laugh. Finna pretended to laugh along. She didn't answer.

She joined the foraging, bridging the spring gap with her eyes and hands. She joined in the care of her siblings' children, starting games and chases, and wearing out her nieces and nephews to the gratitude of their parents.

She inhabited and exhausted her body. She went to bed tired. So tired, all she could do was lounge in the lush greenery, the marble halls, and the gem-latticed caverns, and watch the dancing from silken cushions, massaging her aching legs and shoulders.

When her mother mentioned the guild again—in passing only; she was a woman who knew how to be delicate—Finna heard her. Before she overthought it, she sent a letter to the capital. She had to sell an entire basket of magnolia petal chutney for the postage.

When the request for attendance came, all ribboned and sealed with sky blue wax, Finna had been making jam from a strawberry glut, and her mouth and nose were full of sweet redness. The sugar and letter had mixed within her.

Her mother, who knew nothing about Hewn, cheered and opened last year's cherry wine, and helped Finna pack.

When Finna waved goodbye to her parents, her heart was full of something she couldn't name, and her smile didn't reach her eyes. She tried not to think about how it had been more months since she had seen Hewn than existed between their first and last meeting.

•

As their eyes meet again, Finna wonders how she never remembered there was silver in his navy blue iris.

His eyebrows furrow a little, like a dare. He doesn't speak. He hasn't crossed his arms, but he looks like he wants to.

Options, possibilities, realities flutter past. He may not want her here. He may not want to hear what she has to say.

But she owes it to herself to try.

She lifts her chin again and holds her arms still with her palms facing forward.

She opens her mouth to speak.

•

The guild didn't take anything less than her best. Sleep was carefully, obsessively managed, rationed and observed. Every night, she would travel with a teacher and her classmates, her abilities rigorously tested from every angle. She would inhale bitter smoke before bed. She would be sent on hour-long runs in the evening. She was put on diets of only leaves, then dairy, then starch.

Her teachers refined her abilities, finding her limits, and pushing them back and back and back.

She earned badge after badge. She learned the names of all the variations of liminal and doze. The control came easier and easier.

Yet she didn't try to find Hewn. What if it didn't work? Did she want to try with that risk? She spent her free days picking over the question, over and over like a never-healing scab, staring at it and not asking it, but wanting so much to know the answer.

She finally plucked up the courage to try again. Embedded in a summer, she thought of him and the snow-ornamented trees, of cold air and crunching footsteps, and threw herself into sleep.

The lush jungle filled with birdsong may as well have been a serrated blade.

But, when she wiped away the tears and allowed herself a modest amount of grief, she looked at the question again. She'd learnt that limits could be overcome. She would try again.

She worked harder. She graduated top of her class. She took a job with the guild, taking clients from the wealthy and noble. They paid handsomely for their dreams to be shepherded. She saved for elaborate concoctions to refine her strength in one area, then another.

She tried again. She failed.

She tested every trick she'd learnt. She aimed for snow, she aimed for tall trees. She remembered what the world had smelled like, like salt and blue.

She tried again. She failed.

She travelled to a northern guild, where a scholar was positing that dream worlds overlap with other worlds, that the inhabitants of some could be as real as ours. She remembered how solid Hewn had felt. She remembered how she had called him unreal and false, and the regret was more bitter than even the worst concoction she had been forced to drink.

She tried again. She failed.

She rehearsed what she would say to him when she saw him. She practised apologies and demands, accusations and regrets. Every time she ended up in a place almost like his, every time the similarity only lasted a glance, something inside her broke.

She kept trying. She kept failing.

She sought out obscure texts, untested theories. The clarity of that winter lived inside her like a spotlit gem. She ignored the tempting whisper of failure. Things would be less complicated if she stopped trying. She vowed she would try one last time.

She tried again.

She didn't fail.

•

"I'm sorry," she says. The words come faster than she meant them to. They hang between them like a necklace: beautiful, expensive, heavy. Snow falls around them, a slow, swirling curtain.

Maybe you were wrong to try so many times? What if he's not interested? That winter was so long ago. She'd once wondered about moving on. *He must have done so too?*

She wants to say more, but all the things she wants to say shove and jostle in her mind. *I'm so sorry. I didn't mean most of what I said. I haven't stopped thinking about you. Please trust me. Please tell me you missed me. I missed you.*

But the words get pushed away as he closes the distance between them in two long strides. And she is swept up in his arms, the glance of his skin against hers like sky blue and turmeric, the smell of his neck like the song of an owl, and his words are not so much heard as felt in the vibrations between their bodies.

"I missed you."

Dreaming Crystals

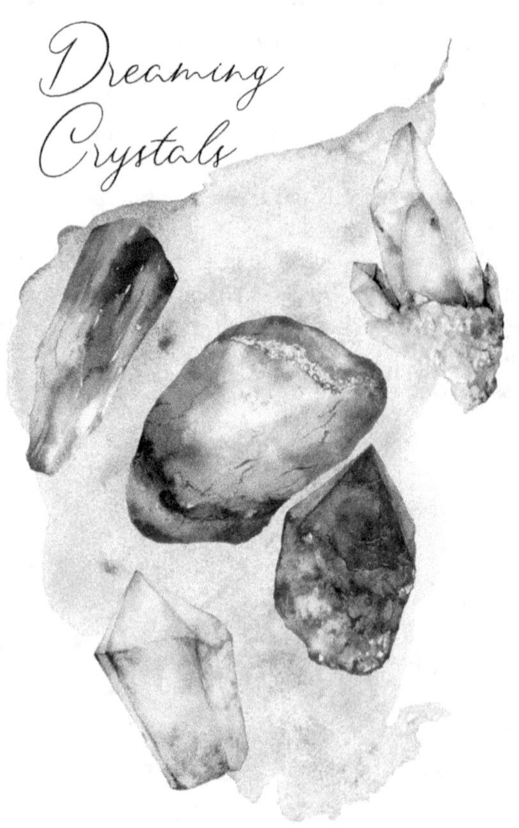

Dreaming Crystals

Not all crystals are for all people. When doing crystal work, it is important to be aware of your senses and respect how your body, mind and energy react. If you feel uncomfortable, anxious, fearful or overwhelmed while working with a crystal, put it aside. It may be better aligned with you another time.

Make sure your clear your crystals often. Especially the darker denser crystals like Tourmaline and Malachite. You can leave your crystal out under moon light, leave them in a bag or box with a piece of clear quartz, smoke cleanse with rosemary or your favorite incense or set them on pieces of selenite. In a pinch, you can use a clear quartz point and hold it to the crystal and simply ask it to clear. With crystals, the intention is half of the process.

Different crystals require different practical care. Some crystals should not get wet. Others should be kept out of the sun. Some are toxic and should be handled with care. Do your own research when choosing how to use and care for your crystals.

Alexandrite is a manifesting stone that stretches the parameters of imagination and promotes bigger, more joyful dreams.

Amethyst is an all-healer and one of the most powerful crystals you can keep. Sleeping with it can assist with astral dreams, intuitive dreams, promoting high vibrations and high frequency dreaming in other planes and energetic bodies.

Bloodstone can go in a bowl of water beside your bed to promote restful sleep, or under your pillow for prophetic dreams. It can be worn continuously to gently ground a tired, overstimulated mind, evoke powerful dreams and provide healing and creativity.

Chalcedony should be worn as jewelry against the skin. This gentle healing stone can balance the mind, body and emotions, soften insecurities and dissipate bad dreams.

Danburite can be placed under the pillow to promote lucid dreaming. It clears auras, carries through large transitions and opens up higher chakras, all while bringing peace.

Jasper can be placed under your pillow to allow you to remember dreams more easily. Black Jasper, or Basanite, can also be used for scrying, or provoking prophetic dreams.

Kyanite is worn as a pendant to enhance meditation, attunement, psychic abilities, and recalling dreams. Kyanite can also help with healing within dreams and align chakras

Labradorite can be kept next to your bed or held over your heart to protect you during dreaming, promote dream travel, and moving into high planes and other worlds during sleep. It promotes calm, rest, balance and gentle processing of problems. It also imparts wisdom and spiritual awakenings.

Malachite is a bit like a live wire and should be used carefully and with consideration and only for a short while. It can used as jewelry or directly on the body in meditation. If at any time you feel off or uncomfortable, remove the stone. It has its time and place. Malachite can be used to enhance intuition, promote intuitive dreams, clear psychic distress and help process information. It can stimulate dreams, and allow you to process old memories and trauma through them in a gentle and transformative way. Don't use it until you are ready to put in the work and go on the journey. Malachite is toxic and should not be consumed in any form.

Moonstone opens up psychic abilities and clear sight, and promotes lucid dreaming. Wear it as jewelry, but be careful during the full moon.

Rhodochrosite gently brings forward repressed feelings, fears and insecurities to be processed and released, enhancing dreams and creativity. Place on heart or solar plexus during meditation.

Ruby helps you follow your dreams. It is a protective stone that blocks psychic and energetic attacks and parasites while provoking powerfully positive dreams. It allows you to observe situations clearly and from a higher state, while attracting in the life you wish for. Wear it as a jewelry.

Tourmaline, particularly rainbow tourmaline stimulates beautiful, joyful dreams that enhance imagination and creativity. It guides healing and spiritual evolution through opening dream doors to the inner and higher selves and high planes. Black tourmaline can protect from nightmares, night terrors and entities that disturb sleep.

The Dreaming of Dibia Snow

BY BELLA CHACHA

The dust came quietly, as it always did.

It came without warning, rolling over the red earth in thin, white sheets. It slipped through open windows and under crooked doors. It settled in hair, on tongues, inside the eyes of children not yet asleep. The elders said it was the ancestors' breath. That the harmattan wind came every year to sweep the world clean of noise and sin.

But that night, the dust came with something else.

Adaobi noticed it first when the goats refused to make noise. The old billy goat, Uka, who never kept quiet, stared at the sky with his mouth shut and his eyes wide. Her grandmother, Mama Eke, had already gone to bed early, muttering about a dry ache in her bones. And the village, once alive with evening voices and pepper-soup laughter, was too still.

"Something is not right," Adaobi whispered, standing on the veranda and staring out into the thickening night.

The moon hung low and yellow above the iroko tree at the edge of the compound. The air smelled like old ashes and dried leaves. She rubbed her arms through the thin wrapper tied around her chest, but the chill was not from the weather.

She stepped inside and went to check on Mama Eke.

The old woman lay on her raffia mat, her chest rising and falling softly, but her lips were parted and dry. A bowl of crushed alligator pepper and chalk sat at the foot of her bed, leftovers from her evening prayers.

"Mama," Adaobi called softly.

No answer.

She bent and touched her grandmother's wrist. Warm. Alive. But something about the way her eyes fluttered behind closed lids gave Adaobi a strange feeling in her stomach.

She walked outside again. The compound was deathly quiet.

She crossed over to the neighbor's hut. She knocked. Waited. Then pushed the bamboo door open.

Inside, the family of four lay on their mats, still as stone.

She ran. From one house to the next. Calling names. Shouting. Knocking.

Nothing.

Not even a cough or groan.

By the time she reached the village square, the dust had thickened into a fine white mist. It coated the wooden drums and scattered stools. It floated in the air like spirit feathers.

Everyone was asleep.

And none of them would wake up.

She returned to Mama Eke's hut just before dawn, heart pounding, feet aching. She sat in the center of the floor, surrounded by silence and old shadows. Her mouth was dry. Her hands trembled.

Then she remembered the box.

Before sleep, Mama Eke had said, *"If the dust dreams too deeply, look inside the box under my mat."*

Adaobi pulled the raffia mat aside. There it was – a carved wooden box, the color of old charcoal. She opened it.

Inside:

A dried kola nut with three cowries pressed into its skin. A small clay gourd with symbols etched along its neck. A scrap of goatskin marked in red ink with her grandmother's spidery handwriting.

She unfolded it and read the note:

"To wake a dreaming world, one must first step into the dream. Do not be afraid. Harmattan remembers. The ukpuru remembers. So must you."

Adaobi stared at the note, then at the items in her lap.

She thought about her grandmother's stories, tales of Onye Nro the dream ones, and the ancient dibia who could walk the sleeping paths. She never believed they were real. But now, as the wind hissed outside and the village lay frozen in sleep, there was no room left for doubt.

She rose slowly, wrapped the gourd in a strip of cloth, and tucked the kola nut into her pocket.

Then she stepped out into the cold gray morning.

The iroko tree waited.

And the dust, now thicker than before, curled around her ankles like a serpent of smoke.

The path to the iroko tree was lined with silence.

Adaobi walked barefoot, holding the gourd tight against her chest. The air stung her cheeks. All around her, the dust floated like ash from a slow-burning fire. Even the birds had fallen quiet. The world felt hollow, as if someone had drawn all the sound out of it with a calabash.

The iroko tree stood alone at the edge of the village, its wide roots curled like sleeping snakes. Its bark was pale and dry, and during harmattan it wept sap that smelled like old wine. Mama Eke once told her it was planted by a dibia who vanished in her sleep and never woke. *"The tree feeds on dreaming,"* she had said. *"That's why it never dies."*

Adaobi placed the gourd, the kola nut, and the goatskin note before the tree. She knelt, trying to recall the rhythm of

Mama Eke's voice when she taught her how to call the gate between worlds.

She drew three circles in the dust, one for the body, one for the spirit, one for the path between them. In the center, she crushed the kola nut and sprinkled its powder into the grooves. The scent of bitter chalk filled her nostrils.

Then she uncorked the gourd.

Inside was a mixture of camwood dust, nzu (white clay), dried bitterleaf, and something darker, something that smelled like rain on old stone. Adaobi dipped two fingers into the thick paste and drew ibie, sacred marks, across her forehead and chest. The designs spiraled inwards like tiny roads.

Finally, she whispered the invocation Mama Eke had made her memorize, though she had laughed at it then.

"Ọnwụ dị n'uzo adịghị egwu dibia nrọ.
Gate of sleep, open. Let me walk where breath cannot reach."
The wind shifted.

The leaves of the iroko trembled.

And the dust around her began to swirl – slow at first, then faster, curling upward into a silent storm.

Adaobi closed her eyes.

And the world fell away.

•

She woke standing.

Not lying, not floating, standing, barefoot, in a forest made of glass.

The trees were tall and silver, their leaves fluttering soundlessly in a wind she could not feel. The sky above was pale blue, but no sun shone there. Instead, a long crack of light split the clouds like a sleeping eye slowly opening.

Adaobi looked down. Her shadow didn't match her movements. When she turned her head, the shadow's head stayed still. When she walked forward, it walked sideways.

"This is not a dream," she said aloud, but her voice came back to her in a whisper from behind.

It wasn't just any dream. This was the Mbido Nro —the Beginning of Dreams.

That Mama Eke spoke of only once, in whispers, when Adaobi was too young to understand.

"There are places under sleep," she had said, *"where the soul walks without the body. The dibia who trained in that place could speak to spirits, bargain with gods, and return with answers no waking eye could see. But the price was never small."*

Adaobi walked through the glass forest, leaves crunching like dry bone under her feet.

Then she saw it.

A figure, tall and masked, standing in the distance.

It wore a white wrapper stained at the hem and carried a staff that flickered like a dying star. The mask was long and hollow, painted with red ochre and the chalky white of funeral rites.

The figure did not move.

But Adaobi's name echoed softly in the air: "Adaobi…Adaobi…"

She stepped forward, heart pounding.

And the forest shifted.

Not just the trees, but the path, the color of the sky, the sound of the wind. Everything turned with her.

Then came the whisper again, this time from the figure.

"You walk where others sleep. But do you remember who waits in the dream?"

Adaobi opened her mouth to answer.

But the dream broke like a mirror under stone.

•

She woke at the base of the iroko tree, gasping.

The gourd was still in her lap. The wind had stopped. The sun had not yet risen, but something in the air had changed. It no longer felt empty.

The dust had settled.

But her hands still trembled.

The figure's voice still rang in her ears.

"Do you remember who waits in the dream?"

•

That night, Adaobi dreamt without sleep.

Her body remained curled beneath the iroko tree, but her soul slipped again into the path of sleepwalkers.

This time, the dream began not with the glass forest, but with mirrors – tall ones, round ones, shattered ones, hanging from the air like moons. She walked among them slowly, barefoot, listening to the sound of her own breath as it echoed across invisible walls.

Each mirror showed a different version of her.

In one, she was still a child, chewing sugarcane beside Mama Eke's cooking fire. In another, she was old and wrinkled, eyes filled with sorrow. In the last, she wore a crown of white feathers and a necklace made of sleeping mouths.

She paused at that mirror.

The mouths on the necklace whispered words she could not understand – sibilant things, like riverwater speaking in its sleep. The feathers in her hair shivered, though there was no wind.

Then, behind her, the soft knock of a staff on stone.

Knock. Knock. Knock.

Adaobi turned.

The masked figure had returned.

Closer now. And taller.

The ochre on its mask ran down like blood tears. The staff it held flickered again – its head shaped like a twin-faced moon. Around its feet, the mirrors melted into puddles of ink.

The voice, when it came, sounded like thunder wrapped in silk.

"Do you know why they sleep?"

Adaobi swallowed hard. "The harmattan. The dust…."

"No. The forgetting. Your people stopped honoring the path of nightwalkers. They buried their dreams in concrete and plastic and noisy prayers that never reach beyond the waking."

The masked figure took one step forward.

"Once, every household had a dream bowl. Once, every child learned the names of the seven gates. Now, they dream without offering. They forget their ancestors. And so, they are forgotten."

Adaobi felt something stir in her chest. Guilt, maybe. Or awe.

The mirrors hissed and reformed into a spiral, forming that led upward into nothing.

"I am Onye Ruo Uka," the being said, tapping the staff once more. "Those who doubt the dream. I wait at the edge of every sleep, but no one visits anymore. So I sealed the village in rest, to remind them what it means to wander the inner forest."

Adaobi dared a question.

"Why me?"

The mask turned slightly. The twin moons shimmered.

"Because your grandmother remembered. And she remembered you."

Suddenly, the mirrors flashed with a new image.

The village, still sleeping, but now the people murmured in their dreams. Whispered fragments of old prayers. Faces softened, fingers twitching.

Some part of them was waking beneath the sleep.

"You are the key," Onye Ruo Uka said. "But the path will cost. To wake them, you must journey to the root of the dream and speak the name that binds this slumber. You must walk until your spirit breaks, and still walk more."

Adaobi's voice shook. "And if I fail?"

"Then they remain here. In the garden of forgetfulness. And in time, even their names will vanish from your tongue."

He turned.

The staircase of mirrors began to pull away, rising like smoke into the sky.

"You have three crossings before the dream hardens. Walk wisely."

And with that, the figure vanished.

·

Adaobi fell, not down, but sideways, through memories, through song, through the voice of Mama Eke calling her name in lullabies half-forgotten.

She landed again in the forest.

But this time, the trees were made of coral. The sky dripped with threads of silk. And the river ahead flowed in reverse.

She took a deep breath and stepped forward.

The dream was alive.

And it was watching.

The river moved backward.

Its waters rippled toward the hills, dragging fish made of ash and birds that sang without sound. Adaobi stood at the edge and watched a canoe carve its way against the current, rowed by no one. The wood was slick with frost, and symbols flickered along its side, faint Nsibidi marks that shifted when she tried to read them.

She stepped into the canoe.

It rocked once, then carried her into the folds of the dream without a paddle, without wind, without time.

Around her, the dreamworld pulsed.

Above, clouds split into the faces of sleeping children. Trees bent to whisper into the water. A deer with seven eyes watched her from the bank, and behind its gaze, Adaobi felt the weight of stories long buried.

"This place knows me," she thought, gripping the edge of the boat. *"Or knows what I could have been, if I hadn't stopped listening."*

Then came the voice.

Not loud this time.

A child's whisper, tucked inside a leaf:

"Who sings the dream of the living, when the dreamers forget their song?"

The boat struck shore.

Adaobi stepped out into a grove that smelled of clay and burnt yam. There, half-covered in vines, stood a shrine carved from saltstone.

A cracked gourd sat in its center.

And beside it, sleeping, was a girl no older than ten. Her hair was braided with cowries. Her mouth twitched as if she were laughing in her sleep. Around her neck hung a charm: a miniature ọfọ staff tied with a strip of red cloth.

Adaobi knelt beside the child.

The girl's eyelids fluttered. Her lips moved.

"Ada… Adao… Adaobi…"

She gasped.

It was her.

Not as she was, but as she had once been, before Mama Eke taught her the first story, before she learned shame for old things, before the world told her to speak only in waking tongues.

The child reached for her.

Adaobi took the small hand.

Their skin met.

And the grove dissolved.

•

She now stood at the gates of a compound wrapped in frost and feathers. Ivory masks hung from every doorway. The sky above turned violet, split with lightning shaped like writing.

A voice boomed, not angry, but heavy with memory:

"You have touched the seed of remembrance."

"Few return to the child-self and emerge whole."

"But now you must choose."

Onye Ruo Uka appeared once more, staff glowing with snowlight.

He raised a hand.

"To wake your people, you must offer the child-self as anchor. That version of you will never return. You will lose your old laughter, your unknowing joy. But the village will remember the dream path again".

Adaobi's chest tightened.

"Is that the cost?" she whispered. "To save them, I must forget her?"

The god said nothing.

Only waited.

The wind curled around her fingers like questions.

And slowly, heart trembling, Adaobi nodded.

The dream cracked like dry clay.

Light surged through the frost-feathered compound, through the river, the coral forest, the staircase of mirrors. Names rushed into the wind, Nneka, Chibundu, Ijeoma, Ekene - each name spoken in a voice long silent.

The dream was waking.

And so was the village.

But Adaobi? She felt the child-self slip from her chest like warm breath on cold air.

She smiled.

And wept.

At first, it was only the wind.

It slipped over the rooftops of Umunne River like a sigh. The kind of wind that carried not warnings or storms, but breath – the deep inhale of something turning, something returning.

The harmattan dust had settled.

The white haze thinned. The brittle leaves softened with dew. Sunlight broke through in narrow shafts, lighting the thatched compounds where people had lain frozen for days.

Then came movement.

Small, slow things. A finger twitching. Toes curling against mats. Heads turning toward familiar smells – ogiri, smoked fish, warm oil.

Adaobi sat alone beside Mama Eke's hut, her legs tucked beneath her. She hadn't moved since the dream let her go.

The silence around her wasn't empty.

It was full – of *becoming*.

One by one, the village stirred.

Old men blinked at the sky like newborns. Children clutched their mothers and babbled fragments of half-remembered dreams. Women stepped into courtyards barefoot, eyes wide with wonder.

They looked at one another, then looked inward.

Each bore the mark of dreaming.

Each had wandered somewhere sacred.

•

Inside the dream, Adaobi had given something of herself, left it behind like a thread in a loom. But here, in the waking world, she felt no emptiness.

Only clarity.

She saw now how rest was not always absence.

Sometimes, it was remembering.

Sometimes, it was a kind of healing the tongue didn't know how to speak.

Mama Eke emerged from the hut behind her. Her back was bent but her eyes gleamed.

"You came back," she said, smiling. "And brought them with you."

Adaobi rose, unsteady but strong.

"They weren't lost," she whispered. "Just asleep beneath forgetting."

Mama Eke nodded. "Then you did it well. You remembered for all of us."

Around them, villagers were gathering. Not to celebrate. Not yet.

But to be still, together.

To sit in that golden hush, where the long sleep had shaken something loose – something old and heavy and hidden.

A kind of weariness was lifting. Not the kind from tired bodies, but from tired spirits. From prayers said too fast. From stories left untold.

They had dreamed.

And the dream had washed them clean.

•

That night, when the fireflies returned, Adaobi sat beside the iroko tree and opened a new gourd, this one painted in the symbols she had seen along the mirror staircase.

She poured libation to the wind.

To the roots.

To the girl she once was.

And in the silence, she felt the village breathe with her.

The dreaming had ended.

But the remembering had only just begun.

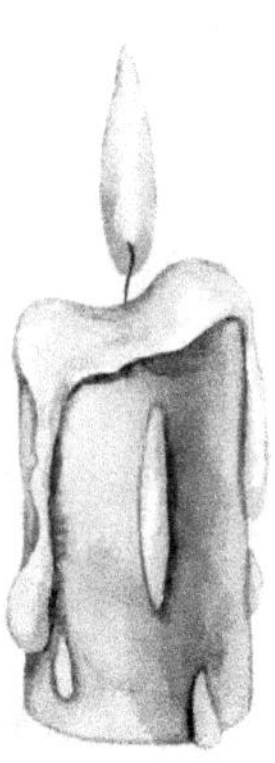

With the woods
wrapped in silence,
I thought they wouldn't hear me coming–

My breath caught in air
cold enough to burn stars,
the only sound in the night that of
the sky slowly turning.

I thought I'd be lucky like this,
surprising creatures in their beds
like a thief.

But they knew better,
this forest much more theirs than mine.

Aurora

My only companions so far have been wraiths
raised by wind, and they're always in a hurry,
running over snowdrifts in pursuit of things
I never seem to see.

There's something out here—
something big and sighing in the darkness,
a heavy hand that slowly creeps down over tree limbs,
ready to snatch you from your sleep.

It isn't safe to stay here,
to dream.

But I'm growing weary,
tired from watching and hoping for company
on this long lonely night.

My head tolls,
and I hope there is safety in numbers,
because I can't go on for much longer.

The stars overhead sit at standstill,
watching me with sharp, old eyes
as I curl up among tree roots.

I send a wordless prayer to Orion
on the wind, my voice lost.

Please watch over me
in my dreams.

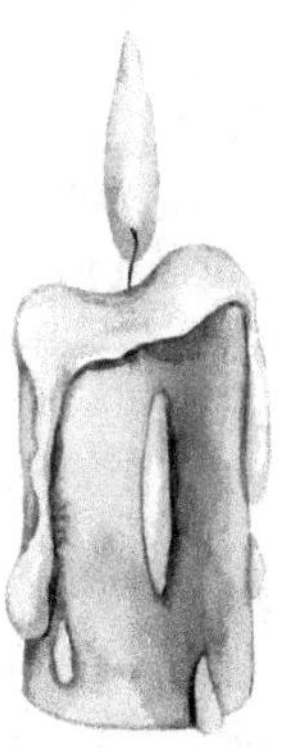

About the Authors

Jordan Bianchi (he/him) is a writer, podcaster, creative producer, and educator based in Buffalo, NY. He loves to write about self-healing, spirituality, and finding one's light through fantasy stories. Jordan is the host of *Aurora Airwaves*, a podcast about creative recovery, artistic discovery, and how we can take care of ourselves while creating art.

In Memoriam

Cheryl Croce Cantafio's first book, *My Stay with the Sisters*, was a collection of poems honoring the journey of grieving a loved one. This was followed by *A Place No Flowers Grow*, a modern-day gothic tale in verse, and *She-Wolf Sonnet*, a nod to the classic monster: the werewolf. Her debut into children's literature was *Barry and the Big Jump*, a story about overcoming one's fears. Cheryl loved being an author and a poet, and she enjoyed meeting readers and local writers like herself at independent bookstores and author events throughout the greater Philadelphia region. Cheryl passed away unexpectedly during the summer of 2025.

Bella Chacha is a writer and poet from Nigeria. Her stories have appeared in Brittle Paper, Cosmic Daffodil, IHRAM Press, Last Stanza, and Heartlines Spec. She was a finalist in the Defenestration 2025 Short Story Contest.

JM Cyrus writes speculative fiction. With a BA in Classical Studies, an MA in Reception Theory, and currently studying for an MFA in Creative Writing, she enjoys finding new worlds, looking at how she found them, and working out how to show them to you. Her work has been published in magazines, anthologies and online.

Kristy Ettel is a female bilingual poet with roots in Australia and Japan, with a Bachelor's degree in linguistics. Her work focuses on the intersection of spirituality, human consciousness, nature, and the animal world.

Clarabelle Miray Fields is a Rhysling-nominated, award-winning speculative writer from Boulder, Colorado, whose work has appeared in *Corvid Queen, Circe's Cauldron*, and elsewhere. She holds a BA in classical languages (*summa cum laude*, 2018) and often writes at the intersection of feminism and ancient myth. She currently serves as editor-in-chief for *Carmina Magazine*, a publication dedicated to modern mythmaking. When not writing, she enjoys being active outdoors, reading, and drinking the darkest coffee she can find.

Jon Negroni Jon Negroni is a Puerto Rican author based in the San Francisco Bay Area. His published books include *The Pixar Theory* (Slimbooks, 2015), a pop culture nonfiction, and his debut fantasy novel *Killerjoy* (5050 Press, 2017). His recent short fiction includes "Men Who Are Strong" (IHRAM Press) and "Upon a Dream," an original fable published in *The Fairy Tale Magazine*. Jon also releases new, original short stories every week on *Cetera Magazine*. He has several upcoming anthology appearances for Neon Hemlock, *Oddity Prodigies, Inked in Gray*, and more. He was also a finalist for the 2025 BCLF Elizabeth Caribbean-American Writer's Prize.

Christina Deason writes under the name CM Riddle. She is an author, creator, mother, grandmamma, and High Priestess. She has published several fiction and non-fiction stories, articles, and books about family, rituals, and magical life experiences. Christina lives with her husband and faithful pets in Sonoma County, CA.

Fendy Tulodo is an art worker from Malang, Indonesia. He works with words and music to study how time feels different to people, and how connections linger even when they're gone. By day, he sells motorcycles. By night, he makes moody music as Nep Kid and writes stories in different forms. His art lives in the gap between words and true feelings.

Nicole Walsh (she/her) is a cat enthusiast from the east coast of Australia who loves fern gardens and long dresses. She writes short and novel-length speculative fiction and urban fantasy that span from a little bit dark, a little bit amusing through to a little bit steamy. Her work features in 30+ magazines and anthologies. Her second novel, sci-fi-fantasy mashup novel *The God-Wife Reborn* is OUT NOW.

Lucy Zhang writes, codes, and watches anime. Her work has appeared in Virginia Quarterly Review, Shenandoah, The Massachusetts Review, and elsewhere.

Check out the other Winter Lore Books:
Yule: Tales for the Winter Solstice
Evergreen: Tales of Winter Shadows

The Collections of Utter Speculation:
The Lost Colony of Roanoke
The Jersey Devil
Lady in White
The Dancing Plague
Cry Baby Bridge
Novellas of Utter Speculation:
Pay the Piper by Sarah Connell
Loading…The Machine Child - March 2026

And our other Books:
Incubate: a horror collection of feminine power
Work in Progress: Story Crafting Notebook
Beach Shorts
Muse
Grimm Retold
Vampire Hunters: An Incomplete Record of
Personal Accounts

www.speculationpub.com